# *Outerborough Blues*

# Outerborough Blues

## A Brooklyn Mystery

## ANDREW COTTO

PUBLISHING

**BROOKLYN, NEW YORK**

Printed in the United States of America
10 9 8 7 6 5 4 3 2 1

Ig Publishing
392 Clinton Avenue
Brooklyn, NY 11238
www.igpub.com


Library of Congress Cataloging-in-Publication Data

Cotto, Andrew.
 Outerborough blues : a Brooklyn mystery / Andrew Cotto.
    p. cm.
 ISBN 978-1-935439-49-3
 1. Brooklyn (New York, N.Y.)--Fiction. I. Title.
 PS3603.O8694O97 2012
 813'.6--dc23
                                          2012006552

*To my wife*

# *Prologue*

My mother's mother came to this country in the usual way—she got on a boat with other immigrants and sailed from Sicily. She wasn't one of them, however: neither tired nor poor or part of any huddled mass. Instead, she traveled alone, with her money in one sock and a knife in the other, coming to the new world with an old world motive—to murder the man that had left her for America.

After searching New York City, every neighborhood in every borough, for him, she traveled by train to anywhere in America that Italians could be found: Boston, Chicago, Kansas City, San Francisco, New Orleans. Back in New York, while waiting for a ship to return home, she met a man, a natural-born citizen whose grandfather had come from the old country to help build the Brooklyn Bridge. She married him and they settled in the Bronx, opening a grocery where Italian housewives bought their meat and pasta and vegetables. In the back of the store, my mother's mother fed the men who had no wives.

My grandparents would have four children—three boys and a girl. Then their boys, all three of them, would die fighting the war in Vietnam. And because of that, my mother's mother took revenge on her husband and daughter; the husband because he had convinced her to stay in America, where so much pain would find her; and the daughter because she was a reminder of her three dead boys. She didn't take her knife to her husband and daughter: instead she cut them with her sharp tongue, kept her distance with dagger stares.

It's no wonder then that my mother ran away with an orphan,

a wild man from Gun Hill Road, where the abandoned and the Irish lived. He was tall and hollow-cheeked, rode a motorcycle and boxed in the amateur ranks. He worked with his hands, building things; and drank with them, too, tearing things down. Despite his moments of violence, he had a sense of humor and a sense of movement, and this was enough to convince my mother to climb on the wild man's motorcycle and escape her wretched home. The young couple moved to the working-class towns of northern New Jersey, where city people in the seventies were buying starter homes and starting families. They would never marry, but would have three boys together. I'm the youngest.

As a family we had no identity, no story, as neither of my parents ever spoke much about their past. Despite this, my mother tried to instill a few traditions in us, like being around the table each night for dinner, though my father would frequently drown that tradition in belligerence and alcohol. I don't know what had happened to him in that orphanage in the Bronx, but when he drank, his eyes often became as hollow as his cheeks, turning from green to gray, and everything after that would be brutal.

While sometimes in a stupor he'd mutter through a veil of unwashed hair about the Irish who raised him so cruelly, it was also that culture that informed his best qualities, particularly the romantic accent and mystical claims. He told truths and he told lies, and it was hard to tell the difference, or if there even was a difference to him. No matter, I listened to every word he said. The man might have been damaged by his past, but he tried to give what he had left to his three boys. So, we learned all about Irish legends, carpentry and uppercuts.

We lived by the railroad, and the trains were with us all day and night—the clanging and whooshing, the warning of the whistle, and the ding, ding, dinging as the safety gates went down. The neighborhood kids made a fortress of the boxcars beside the tracks. We jumped from rooftop to rooftop, chased each other under the bellies, and found warmth or shade within the walls of the abandoned cars.

The moving trains entertained us in a different way. From the cover of trees, we'd hammer the commuter with rocks as it whipped past. The freight trains, slow and unmanned, made for another game altogether. We'd pace our steps alongside the wobbling cars, and with a hand on the ladder, we kept running until our weight rose above the screaming wheels and our legs dangled and groped for the safety of a rung. Then we'd climb aboard and disappear in the distance like a snake into the woods, riding the straight rails on the swath of open land cut through the stretches of never-ending pines, under the open sky in the rattle and rush of movement and freedom. We'd eventually hop off, and on the walk home, down the same tracks from which we'd come, we'd talk about disappearing one day for real.

One day when I was twelve, my father grabbed my wrists in the backyard and told me through his thick, whiskey breath that my brothers and I were nothing more than a mongrel-mix that made us Woppi Indians from the Ghoomba Tribe. He didn't hide his brown toothed smile, but I wanted to believe him, so I did. By genetic good fortune, I grew up tall, dark-haired, and severe-cheeked as an Indian chief. To complete the picture, I braided my hair and wore a bandanna around my head, and in the summer, walked around without a shirt, rubbing the sun-burn into my skin. One time, at a flea market, I stole a buck knife, which I kept tucked in the back pocket of my jeans. I spent hours with that knife, snapping it into place, mastering the handle, sharpening the blade and burying the point, over and over, into the bulls-eye of the box car where I hid.

That was the same year that my father, without a word or

warning, disappeared, leaving my mother alone to raise three boys. The oldest, Sallie, was thick and vicious. He claimed the house and ruled with rage, his presence like an angry dog as he bullied our mother and broke her heart on a regular basis. He reserved a special contempt for me, frequently bashing me with his brick-like fists and steel-toed boots. It was from Sallie that I hid in those boxcars. And it was to protect myself from him that I'd stolen that knife, learned to use it, and always kept it close.

My other brother, Angie, was a derelict prince. All the kids by the tracks followed him because he was cool and tough and smarter than the rest of us. He was the first to hop a train, and the first to take the blame when our delinquent stunts went wrong. Girls followed him, too, mostly home from school, and it was there, at home, that he served as a savior for me. Despite my knife, I couldn't have kept my oldest brother away without Angie's protection.

Because of this, the summer I turned fifteen, when a fight spilled onto the tracks and a commuter train killed my prince of a brother, I had no choice but to leave. So, on an August morning, I hopped a freight car and scaled my way inside. With my knife in one pocket and my money in the other, I rattled to Pittsburgh. I could pass for eighteen then, tall as I'd become, and found work and shelter soon enough, though I didn't stay in Pittsburgh long. I didn't stay anywhere too long. Over the next few years, I worked mainly in restaurants or bars, or building houses. I slept with waitresses and drank with cooks and carpenters, but after a while, I had to move on. And then I had to move on again. In each new place I'd find a job, a roof, the library, and a mailbox. During off-hours from work, I'd sit in the church-like quiet of the public library and learn the missing lessons from my education: literature, history, and the like. I'd study architecture and carpentry and cook books too.

At least once a week, I would write a letter home to my mother. I thought of her every day, at every meal, but I knew that the sound of her voice would be too much to bear, so I wrote her letters, which she always answered. Writing became our ritual. It's how she remained my mother, and how I stayed her son.

My mother had never traveled, so she'd ask me to describe each city I was in; to make her not only see the buildings and the people, but to also feel and hear and taste their lives. Through words, I'd send her the city I was in, from the streets to the sky. I'd observe the people in their routines—what they ate and drank, how they dressed and talked, how they fought and kissed.

One day, a letter arrived from my mother while I was staying in Louisiana, outside Lafayette, in a two-room shack behind a roadhouse. I worked in the kitchen and stayed with the owner's daughter, a Bayou child named Carmen with corkscrew hair and green-apple eyes. She taught me to Cajun jitterbug and cook Creole. The pockets inside her collarbones bubbled with moisture when we danced or made love in the jacket of tropical heat. Some nights we'd walk into the woods, lie on the banks under a canopy of live oak and Spanish moss, and fuck without fear of snakes or demons.

Afterward, in the hard smell of the swamp, as heat lightening flashed and animals died in the distance, we'd suck cigarettes and blow smoke at the yellow moon beyond the trees. I would have liked to stay there for awhile, with Carmen, but the letter from my mother brought me home. She told me that Sallie had been locked up and that she'd die soon.

Back home in New Jersey, I watched my mother waste away from cigarettes and sadness. From her bed, as her legs swelled and her shoulders shrank to nothing but skin and sockets, she spoke—for the very first time—of our family history: the building of the Brooklyn Bridge and her father the American, the grocery he opened with my mother's mother who abandoned her homeland for revenge, and the inheritance of suffering she had handed to her husband and her daughter and her three dead boys, Salvatore, Angelo, and Caesar. With my mother's dry fingers like ribbons on my wrist, she spoke of her dead brothers then wailed over the fate of her three boys, Salvatore (Sallie), Angelo (Angie), and me, Caesar.

My mother, superstitious as she was, begged me to break the curse on the family started by revenge. Her mother had brought the bad spirits with her from Sicily, and they were with us like blood and breath. From her dying heart, she begged me to save myself from suffering, to break the chain of agony it extended. The curse was cradled by movement, she said, and all the bad that had happened to our family was because people ran away, trying to escape this curse. She asked me to stop running, to find a home. I promised her I would. And then I buried her alone. I received the little bit of money she had, and the house, with Sallie in jail, was mine, too, but I couldn't stay there, not with so much misery within those walls and Angie's ghost on the tracks nearby.

With the house boarded up I traveled to the city, arriving like an immigrant from the old world. Manhattan felt too confined after all that time on the open road, so I walked the bridge an ancestor had come here to build, determined to find a home in the mysteries of Brooklyn. The once-proud borough had become an anonymous land of strange faces and tongues, an alphabet soup of subway lines that extended far into forgotten zones. I walked its streets, rode the trains above and below ground. Neighborhoods were there to be discovered—each with their own separate story.

I eventually found a neighborhood where the sky was wide above the carved cornices of four-story brick and brownstone buildings that held fire escapes suspended over sidewalk store-fronts. A business offered hand-made hats, large and colorful. On the corner, a dread-locked man sold drinks in coconuts to school kids in uniforms. Hair salons and barbershops were two-to-a-block. The smell of southern food mingled with the music that came from canted porticos and open car windows. Traffic eased like the slow-walking women whose hips moved nearly as far sideways as their bodies did forward. The men glided along, shiny with confidence. The early evening streets filled with these graceful women and stylish men; surfaced from the subway with the skyline in sight but Manhattan left behind. They touched each other as they spoke, on elbows and wrists, on tree-lined streets with landmark brownstones aligned in formation like an architect's army.

Rippling down from the neighborhood's height were areas of increasing despair. At the far end, in the flats, a long shut-tered navy yard bordered the East River. Up the slope, between the Navy Yard and a big green park, were projects, clusters of short-stack buildings the color of ash. Above Myrtle Avenue, the litter-strewn thoroughfare that severed the projects from the park, were in-between streets, where the houses were historic, but the conditions reflected a different history—a history, in some ways, like mine, of turbulence and the desire to overcome. All through the neighborhood, high and low, the majority of the people didn't look like me—they were black and I was whatever, but that didn't matter because I was alone.

On a quiet, tree-lined block, closer to the navy yard than the heights, I bought a crumbling clapboard of four stories pinched between two brownstones. I worked on the building all sum-mer as the neighborhood kids chalked the sidewalks out front, jumped rope and rode bikes, and played games into the fad-ing light of supper time. Afterward they would return to their stoops to lick ice-cream and holler until the sky turned indigo above the tree line and the adults—who were always out front and knew all the kid's names—called everyone in when the street lamps blinked on.

Through the night, lights blazed inside the open windows of my empty house as I hammered and plastered and painted past August and into autumn. And before the trees lost their leaves and darkness came in the afternoon, I had finished. I bought a few pieces of furniture and decorated the best I could, but the echoing house didn't feel like a home, and because of my wandering nature, I had to live outside my door. So I searched the streets for a job and found one soon enough, once again working for someone else in someone else's bar, unaware at the time that the past was something I could never escape.

*Monday*

The place where I worked was on the ground floor of a brown-stone, on a busy block dedicated to commerce. There were other places to eat and drink, up and down the street of small businesses, places that catered to a variety of tastes and ages, places that came and went, but the place where I worked seemed somehow bigger than the others, dug deeper into the neighborhood's core. The Notch was an old-school joint with old-school rules. They were hung on the wall:

**No Gambling**
**No Fighting**
**No Credit—DON'T ASK!**

Though nobody asked for credit anymore, and there probably hadn't been any dice or punches thrown at The Notch in a generation, the sign still stayed up, right by the door, where everyone could see. It had been hung by the original owner in 1962, and kept in place by his son, the man now in charge, a man who preferred both the past and the power of his own rules.

The Captain sat at the end of the bar, smoking a cheap cigar, studying the names instead of the numbers listed in his ledger. Before opening each weeknight for dinner, the Captain raised the riot gate to half-mast in the afternoon and did business at the end of the bar under a conical light. Neighborhood people in the know—and in the need—ducked under the gate and had a seat next to the burly and paternal Captain, speaking in low voices under the low ceiling. Sometimes the Captain slipped behind the red curtain in back and returned with an envelope, exchanged for a name to be scribbled in the ledger.

I always arrived at four o'clock, and during the hours that the Captain did business, I kept busy at the front of the bar with my four-inch buck knife, dissecting fruit as the stereo played. During its official hours of business, The Notch played a mixture of R&B and soul, even some gospel when the church ladies came by. However, during the unofficial hours of business when the Captain did his business, we played the blues. The Captain and I shared a love of that music, though we never spoke of why. We didn't speak much at all, aware as we were of our roles, so it took me by surprise that particular Monday when the Captain called out my name and jabbed his cigar towards the door.

A white girl, young and hesitant, slipped under the gate and crossed through the sunlight of the sunken room. She had walked by on the sidewalk at least three times in the last fifteen minutes, pausing by the door each time. I was hoping she wouldn't come in because I didn't want to have to kick her out. She stood across the bar's curve, her hands tucked out of sight, her shoulders pinched as if she had failed, while dressing, to separate hanger from garment. Slender in the angled light, with skinny arms and propped-up breasts, she blinked and breathed, hugging herself inside a black knit sweater-dress that crossed her thighs. A bare knee buckled toward the other and black boots covered her calves. Dark hair framed a pretty face splattered with brown freckles as big as milk chocolate snowflakes. Her wide eyes were rimmed with red and I thought of tears until she sneezed. She looked out at the sidewalk where white petals gathered like confetti. The fruit trees that lined the neighborhood streets blossomed early with white flowers that made the branches, for a week or so, seem snow-dusted on the otherwise bare avenues. The petals fell in the steady breeze of spring, filling the air with allergens. The girl sneezed again. I handed her a cocktail napkin.

"Thank you," she whispered in a fragile accent.

"We're not open," I said. "Come back in an hour."

She sat down and ordered a Pastis.

"Not open," I said, a little louder. "You can come back later."

She glanced over her shoulder at the raised gate and ordered again.

Beneath his boating cap with an anchor-insignia, the Captain's fleshy face, purple as a plum, dark around the eyes and gray around the temples, grew amused. He puffed his cigar and blew a cloud into the light over his head.

Finally, the girl spoke. "I have age!" she insisted. "Look! Look!" From a ragged satchel she scattered items across the bar: a compact, a pack of cigarettes, a battered five dollar bill, and a French-English dictionary. She shoved a maroon passport in my direction.

"That's not the problem," I said. "We're not open until…"

"Pour the lady a drink, Caesar, on the house," The Captain cut me off, his voice deep as a drum.

"You sure?" I asked.

"Course I'm sure," he said with a touch of scorn as he stepped from his stool, adjusted the lapels of his navy blue jacket, and vanished behind the curtain in back.

"You are Caesar?" she asked, tilting her head.

"Yeah," The Captain bellowed from out of sight. "Like the salad!" His laughter trailed down the hall and disappeared behind a door. That was the only joke we shared, though I didn't find it all that funny.

"Caesar Salad?" the girl asked me. Her voice, now playful, echoed off the wood-paneled walls.

"Caesar Stiles," I said.

"I prefer *la salade nicoise* to Caesar salad," she said with a wink.

"You don't say," I answered.

She swiveled on the stool and crossed her legs, flashing the soft flesh above her knee.

"No Pastis," I said.

"OK," she said. "Champagne then."

"We have Prosecco," I told her. "It's like Champagne, but from Italy."

"OK, yes," she said. "Champagne, but from Italy."

I filled a flute and placed it in front of her. She pushed the battered five towards me. I pushed it back. After a few sips from her glass, and slow nods of her head to the music, the girl turned her eyes towards the bar. She fingered the soft-pack of cigarettes and lifted a filter-less smoke. I gave her a light. She straightened on the bar stool, the cigarette held out high and to the side in a sophisticated pose. She made for some sight: child-like freckles, grown-up legs, cigarettes and mystery.

In a slow and awkward fashion, with her eyes on me, she brought the cigarette to her pursed lips. She opened her mouth and took in the filter, somehow managing to shoot the cigarette through her fingers and onto the bar. It sparked on the mahogany before rolling to a stop in front of me. The girl lurched off her stool, but I beat her to the cigarette and dropped it in the sink. Her fantastic face flushed with shame.

"Anything else?" I asked, ready to get back to my chores.

"I need help," she whimpered.

As I held her stare, she collapsed into a slouch.

"What's that?" I asked.

"I need help," she repeated, removing her chin from her chest.

I crossed my arms. "What kind of help?"

"To finding someone."

I laughed out loud and looked for the Captain, thinking he might come barreling out from back, holding his side and smiling. A little laugh between me and him, the old crime novel set-up where a desperate girl walks into a bar. Why else would he let a white girl drink for free at his bar during off-hours? The whole thing seemed scripted. But the Captain had rarely laughed with me before, and he didn't come out from behind the curtain then. I was alone with this strange girl and her strange request, and that made me nervous.

I started to suspect that someone might have sent her. I had thought of late that I was being followed. The same car, a blue Chrysler with dented fenders and Jersey plates, had been outside The Notch last weekend; the day before, the same car had been parked around the corner from my home. And this morning, a pile of cigarette butts lay outside my gate, as if someone had spent a good amount of time in front of my house, waiting and smoking. I wasn't sure what to think. Long periods of isolation had left me afraid at times, for no reason. I had no proof that someone was after me, only observation and intuition and a reason, as of late, to be truly afraid. I'd done something stupid, you see, something stupid that could easily get me killed. The man I'd betrayed was the most dangerous type, a living ghost with no history and no name, but still a killer. I called him the orange man because of his manufactured appearance—a comical glow, more like burnt cheese than a sun tan—but nothing about the orange man was funny. I knew he'd come for me at some point, so I had to keep my eyes open and consider every unusual event. And this girl at the bar certainly counted as unusual.

"Where you from?" I asked her.

"South of France," she said, after a long sip. "You know?"

"Yeah, I know," I said. "It's in the south of France."

"You speak French, no?"

"A little Creole," I shrugged.

"Ouf!" she spat. "That is non French."

I went back to slicing fruit, but couldn't ignore her for long, triangulated as I was by regret and curiosity and fear.

"Let me ask you something," I said, spinning the knife between my fingers until the blade was a blur. "What are you doing here?"

Her eyes flashed and her back straightened for an instant before she slumped down like a beaten boxer on a corner stool.

"I told you," she whimpered. "I need help."

"Yeah, I heard that," I said. "But this is a bar."

"Yes, I know," she said, "but people at bar, these places, they know things."

"Want me to read you the menu?" I asked. "Tell you tonight's special? That I know."

She sneezed again and then looked towards the plate glass window where the sinking sun cast shadows over the tables and chairs. The room twinkled with dust particles floating in the afternoon light. Nothing here, except my isolation and the girl; her face was the same but her glass was empty. I filled her up.

Just then, The Captain came from out behind the curtain, cleared his throat and nodded towards the small kitchen up the stairs in back. No more time for the girl. I pulled my long hair into a ponytail and lit a smoke of my own. Leaning into the bar, I smoked and listened to Muddy Waters "Roll & Tumble" as the French girl sulked and sipped her sparkling wine. I studied her, considering all the possibilities, but I couldn't come up with an answer. I thought about leaving right there and then, but then I remembered the promise I had made to my dying mother. I wasn't going to run anymore. So I looked across the bar at a pretty girl and a little bit of mystery. My life could use both. I wrote directions to my house on a cocktail napkin and told the girl to meet me in the morning.

After she left, a single thought stayed with me the rest of the night, a single thought that overwhelmed everything else: if the girl was for real, she had chosen me to help her find someone who was lost. And if I could help her find someone who was lost, it would prove that I wasn't lost anymore, and that I was finally home. And if I was home, the family curse would be broken. It was farfetched and fantastic, I knew, but, just like when my father told me that our family was a mongrel-mix that made us Woppi Indians from the Ghoomba Tribe, I wanted to believe, so I did.

And that's how it started: Monday, the first week in April, six days to Easter. By Sunday, it would be over.

**

Dinner at The Notch that night, like so many nights, was like a planned party: Work attire was relaxed by loosened collars and sleeves rolled to the elbow; hair came down and skin was exposed by buttons opened to air; hats stayed on. Drinks flowed and a steady hum hovered above the tables. An occasional burst of laughter cut through the clamor and smoke, circled the ceiling then escaped out the door. A "jump" record spun as Louie Jordan, with his horns and rhythm, stomped high-energy blues through the speakers. From my coop of a kitchen up the stairs, I pumped out plates and stole glances at the scene below. The Captain, at a table by the front window, watched the room move all through the night.

During a pause in the dinner rush, I took a smoke out on the sidewalk and watched the sky above the rooftops turn midnight blue. Returning through the restaurant, I was called by the church ladies to their rectangular table in the middle of the room. "Young man, young man," the woman at the head cried. A silk dashiki covered her shoulders and matching blue material wrapped her head. Her long brown fingers held my wrist. "Young man," she said with sturdy warmth, "please tell us how you do what you do with this food." The reverend from the local Baptist church and her deacons had been coming in once a week since I had started working here. They were a joyous and dignified group, and their order was always the same: six of anything.

The menu was a blend of Italian traditions and the American south. They liked that. And they liked it more when I ran down each plate: *Pollo Fritto*, a take on fried chicken, sizzled in olive oil; southern-style mac and cheese re-imagined as *Quatro Formaggi*, a three-cheese combo of coated pasta crusted with Parmasean. "Hmm-hmm!" the reverend said to that one. There was *Peposa*, my version of meat loaf, a ground meat mixture thick with tomato paste, onions and garlic, with slabs of bacon on top. The women laughed and nudged each other as I spoke of the ribs being rubbed with spices then slow roasted and glazed with a balsamic reduction. "I'm not sharing these!" the deacon sitting in front of that dish declared. In place of ham hocks was *Cotocino*, the shin of the pig de-boned and stuffed with sausage, herbs and bread, sliced wide and layered over lentils. "Stop!" someone begged. The women were now falling over themselves, about ready to burst. Finally, the reverend had that night's special—fried lamb chops with a dollop of anchovy sauce on the side. "Mmmm-hmmm!" she testified as heads bobbed down and back up again. "Thank you, young man," she said kindly. "Thank you for everything." Then the church ladies held hands above the table, forming a circle. And when they bowed their heads to pray, I walked away, even though I would have liked to join them.

**\*\***

After dinner, with the kitchen clean and dark, I went down to the bar. Everyone had left except the Captain and Jacqui, the new bartender with the cartoon figure. She could hardly fix a drink, but her logic defying combination of curves and straights had them two-deep at the bar even on a Monday night.

I sat on a stool and ordered a Harvey Wallbanger. The night before, I had asked for an Alabama Slammer; night before that, a Side Car. Jacqui shifted her hips and clamped her narrow waist on each side. Her breasts lunged like guard dogs, while her straight face dared me to say another word. Looking at me deadpan, she scratched at her cleavage with a press-on nail, snapped her gum.

"How about a beer, then?" I asked. Jacqui smirked and rolled her eyes.

The Captain remained at his table by the front window. He had company, a thin-limbed lady half his age with a sway back and a gap between her front teeth. She wore her hair in a full blown afro. I liked her style, and we exchanged smiles whenever we passed one another, though I had never caught her name, and imagined I never would. You see, at The Notch, I was the help. People knew who I was, as I was a different color than most as well as being responsible for the new menu, but their desire to know more about me ended there. Also, being exacting about how my food was prepared and served didn't exactly endear me to my co-workers.

Despite the lack of camaraderie, I liked working at The Notch, as the food was good and the scene even better. From my perch up on high, I watched the floor every night, and, on certain evenings, I could feel the constant energy of a community, which was the best a restaurant could hope for. When dinner was over, and my work for the night had ended, I'd sit at the bar and recall how I had ended up there.

For months, I'd been alone in my new home, and a feeling of deep loneliness was dripping like a leak. I worked out most days, devoured books and took long turns around and around the borough and rest of the city. On nice days I walked; on not so nice days, I traveled by train. Parched leaves scratched the sidewalk and the city and its neighborhoods began to fade into winter. A cold wind picked up, and I envisioned a long period of solitude, which would not serve me well. So, on a gray, biting afternoon, I stepped into The Notch for shelter and a beer.

"The Blues Hour" played from a jazz station out of Newark as I sipped a stale stout from a tap in need of cleaning. The only one in the place was the Captain, heavy-set and harried, struggling through prep, hacking up fruit, clambering to-and-from the back with buckets of ice, cases of beer, all the while cursing some *no good God-damn mother-fucker* who must have left in him in this lurch. There were cartons of booze stacked all around the front room, full ashtrays, and a broken broom in the corner. The small, open kitchen up the stairs was dark. Despite his frenzy, the Captain paused every now and then, squinting above the bar at speakers that leaked a static of crying stings and moaning vocals. At one point, he removed his cap and scratched his head.

"Elmore James," I said.

"What's that now?" he asked, startled, as if he had forgotten I was there.

"You were wondering who that is?" I motioned with my head towards the speakers.

"Yeah," the Captain said, straightening from a hunch on the side of a bar that a man of his size and stature was on the wrong side of. "The hell is that?"

"Elmore James."

"Right, right, Elmore James." he said, snapping thick fingers.

"Thanks for the help, my man." He tipped his cap, and went back to work, a little consternation removed from his weary face.

I watched him struggle for a while longer.

"You need any help?" I finally asked.

"What's that now?" he winced, palming the small of his back.

I sipped my beer and looked around the room.

"Looks like you could use some help."

He studied me for a cold minute, then took a look around the room himself.

"Ain't that a..." he muttered. "You know anything about the bar business, son?"

"Just a little," I said, frowning at the bad excuse for a beer in front of me.

He stepped away from the bar.

That was six months ago, and in that time I'd done everything I could to make myself indispensable: I'd taken over the kitchen and introduced a new menu; I opened and closed the place six nights a week; prepped the bar and the kitchen; ordered all the food and booze; poured drinks on Saturday afternoon when no one else wanted to work. I practically lived at The Notch, though it didn't feel like home until that French girl walked in and asked me for help.

**

In the open sky above the hushed streets, the moon was a porcelain plate on a black table as I walked home. A breeze raised the collar of my jean jacket as I sliced through the silvery silence, past unlit buildings and quivering trees and cars idle by the curb. The air felt like glass. I crossed empty corners under the mauve light of overhead lamps. Just me and the moon until a clacking sound picked up, approached, and passed in the figure of a boy on a bicycle. He circled around and me and crossed the other way. Then he came back for another pass, like a stray cat tangling around my legs, and kept going as I emerged from tree cover and rejoined the moon to turn up my block.

I knew him as the third of three brothers who lived across the street from me in a cracked Victorian row house. He was small and awkward and always alone. He read comic books under the crumbling portico and rode around in the middle of the night on a rusty three-speed bike, a baseball card held to the spokes by a clothespin. We met like this most evenings on my way home from work. I never knew if he was just passing or wanted my attention. Either way, I couldn't wonder about him that evening, as I had other things to consider:

On the sidewalk in front of my gate, the pile of cigarette butts, scattered like slain soldiers, had grown larger. The street was empty, but someone had been there for another half packs' worth of waiting. I sat on the wooden steps and considered the possibilities. None of them were good. As a jet soared overhead, the past came rushing back to me. I lit a cigarette and remembered when I ran away from home.

I made it to Pittsburgh in a day on the train and spent the night at a makeshift camp by the junction. Hobos and drifters gathered around fires and moaned in the dark. I slept with the knife in my hand and yet still got beat up in my sleep. When the morning came, I was bruised and broken, missing my money, my knife, and one shoe.

I crossed a river into downtown. The buildings were modern and the streets open and empty during the early morning hours. I entered a warehouse district with antique streets and stores. People were sympathetic and smiled as I hobbled past. Over the next couple of days, a few strangers gave me money or something to eat. But still I had to steal to survive. From neighborhood markets I lifted bread and cheese and hunks of dry meat. In parks, I carved meals with a knife I'd pocketed at a pawn shop.

After three weeks on the street, sleeping under bridges along the river, turning cups of coffee into makeshift showers in restaurant bathrooms, I found a place to live with two brothers from the Dominican Republic. I was stealing food from a garbage dumpster outside a diner in the Strip District one night when a man suddenly snatched me by the arm, yanked me inside the clanging and sweltering kitchen, threw me an apron, and pointed towards a stuffed sink. He yelled something to a brown man standing there. The man smiled at me and shook loose a cigarette. After we scrubbed and dried a few thousand dishes, glasses and utensils, he brought me to his apartment around the back of a large building, where he lived with his older brother, who did maintenance for the building and also got the only bed in the three-room basement unit. I slept on the floor, next to the younger brother who slept on a couch with the springs and stuffing coming out. The boiler raged in the room next door and a thin stream of air came through a trap window. Water bugs crawled on me all night, but it was better than being outside, wondering if I'd get killed in my sleep.

The diner where I now worked was open twenty-four hours a day, and was manned by a mash of immigrants. The menu was thick as a phone book, and on any given day, at any given time, you could have a row of line six cooks from six continents cranking out food from six countries. From these men, I would learn how to fry and sauté, roast and braise, as well as how to mix seasonings and make marinades and brines. I observed that, despite their country of origin, many recipes contained the same basic ingredients.

The dishwashers and maintenance crews added to the jumble of languages and hues. The waitresses were all Korean school girls who called the owner Uncle. Uncle was a wrinkled and stooped Korean man of about fifty. He wore cardigan sweaters and khakis, and a pair of reading glasses hung from his neck on a metal chain. A buzz saw of sound and motion, he did most of his talking with his hands and kept them flailing on his endless rounds through the diner. Sometimes he would grab a cleaver or a mop from an employee to demonstrate exactly what he wanted.

"You work hard!" he said to me one day after a few weeks on the job. At first I didn't know if he was paying me a compliment or giving me an order. Then he took me by the wrist and led me to the long prep table, where I stood before a pile of vegetables and next to a small Ethiopian man who nodded at a massive knife. The move from the dishes to the plates was a promotion, but the pay was the same. Pay was the same for everyone in the kitchen, and Uncle doled out the cash every Friday afternoon. Since I couldn't get a bank account and didn't feel safe storing cash anywhere, I'd take my pay to the Western Union office and wire most of it home to my mother.

I worked roughly seventy hours a week, and had every other Sunday off. Every other Saturday night, the Dominican brothers would take me to a barber shop in the Hill District that was closed on the street side and open around back. Inside, men and women, all various shades of brown, crammed into a back room lined with card tables. Food in foil—roasted pork, beans and rice, fried platanos and mashed yucca—steamed on every table. In the corner was a metal garbage can filled with green beer bottles floating in ice beside a table with a bottle of Brugal and small paper cups.

From their billfolds, the men pulled worn pictures of skinny children, barefoot and barely dressed—their families back home. They chased their stories of longing with shots of rum and hand-rolled cigarettes. The women around them were in high demand. After tending to the food, they swung their bodies through the room and took partners toward the music up front in the barber shop. These women called me *Yunior* and treated me like a child, pinching my cheeks and giving me plates piled with food.

I'd usually stay in back with the men, listening to arguments in Spanish about baseball and politics. Late in the evening, after the crowd had thinned, I'd go up front, sit in a barber chair, dizzy from drink and full of food, and watch couples move in a way that was beyond comprehension. There was order, but instinct. The women shook their shoulders and kept time with their soft bellies and swinging-bell asses, their smooth brown skin reflecting the barber's bright light, while the men never hid their compulsions but managed to stay composed. Sometimes, when the smoke was thick and my head thicker, it would seem like they were all floating.

Even after falling asleep, I could still feel the rumba of the music. At some point near morning, the younger brother would find me sprawled across a barber's chair. "*Muchacho*," he'd say, his face smiling and alive, his shirt unbuttoned and ruffled. "Is time to go." We'd then walk home through the dark and empty streets, eating loaves of still warm bread just delivered to restaurant vestibules, as spots of light appeared in the early dawn.

I threw my cigarette on the pile of butts and spat on the sidewalk. The street was silent. Whoever was waiting for me was not coming back tonight. So I went into my empty house, felt my way through the darkened parlor and up past the second floor landing to the stairs that led to the loft, where I fell asleep in my clothes.

**

I dreamed of Carmen in the moonlight of the bayou. She ran through curtains of moss towards smoky light, before vanishing behind gum trees. I could hear her breath but not find her face. Then she giggled and trampled the undergrowth. Through the smell of night-blooming flowers, we raced towards the fake light of dawn and a horizon swimming with starlings. But in the clearing there was no Carmen, only saw grass and fish heads and dead cypress trunks. And me, alone on the banks of the bayou, brown water rising above my shoes.

I woke up soaked in sweat, sensing that disparate elements around me were about to collide.

*Tuesday*

The back window of my bedroom looked out over a garden. In the yard directly below, sunlight splashed through the trees and covered Angel, my tenant, in the mid-morning light. Within the latticed fence, she planted flowers around the border of a slate patio. After watching her for a few minutes, on her hands and knees with a small trench shovel digging holes in the dirt that she filled from a basket of bulbs, I went downstairs in jeans, t-shirt and bare feet. Through the parlor and the open kitchen, I unlocked the back door, which opened to a wrought-iron terrace. Wild ivy wended in through the openings and clutched the black iron. I picked off a thread and it snapped upon release.

"Oh, hi, Caesar," Angel said, turning to notice me. She swiped her brow with a thin wrist and stripped off her gardening gloves. I stood in the shade of a Locust tree that listed from the neighbor's yard. Angel was below in the sunlight, her dark, reddish skin glowing with the amber energy of burning sugar. Her braided hair rested on the shoulder straps of faded overalls.

"Skipping school today?" I asked. Angel was a second grade teacher at a public school down the slope.

"No school this week, Caesar," she said with a toothless smile. "It's spring break. I figured I better get these flowers in the ground before the rain comes on Saturday." Angel always knew the weather, and it was pretty much all we talked about during our infrequent conversations. She had lived downstairs for nine months, but we were hardly ever saw one other. She had come from DC, fresh out of graduate school, ready to take on the public schools of New York City. My money was on her, as she had an aura of invincibility, the kind that I'd noticed in certain women, especially of color. Before renting the ground floor apartment, she had asked for access to the backyard in exchange for tending to the garden. I would have given her the whole house if she wanted it. As it was, she stayed downstairs and I remained above. We kept very different hours, and very different lives, but I always felt her presence and wondered, with every thudding footstep through the parlor, if she was aware of mine as well. I also wondered about Easter, as The Notch would be closed and I had a leg of lamb and some old wine to share.

"What do you think of the garden so far?" she asked.

I told her it looked just fine, even though the only things coming from the soil were the thick tips of something green and a couple of clamped tulip bulbs. She went back to work and spoke to the earth. "When everything comes up it will be beautiful. I promise."

In another yard a few fences down, a Magnolia bloomed with pink and white petals, its fragrance sweet on the breeze. A Koi pond gurgled out of sight. The neighbor directly behind—a stooped, aged man—limped to the coop that bordered our fence. His pigeons flocked to the roof of the shed, milled and pecked for a few moments, before bursting into flight. Up in the sky, the birds followed the direction of a long pole with a garbage bag for a mast that the man struggled to wave. Their faint-brown top feathers sparkled pink as they swooped from the shade into the light. When flipped, their white bellies glowed golden in the open sky. They looped and looped, from shade to light and back again. Then the pole stopped swinging and the birds returned home. They pecked around the roof and fluttered into their coop. The old man ambled back inside.

Before I left Angel to her backyard and flowers and promise to make things beautiful, I paused to look up at my house, checking the surface for cracks, the gutters for sag, the window frames for rot. Everything was in good condition, but the listing tree from next door loomed over me, as if it could come crashing down with only the slightest provocation.

**

Out front, the breeze stirred soft applause from new leaves. The branches of a Sycamore across the street swayed, its shadow dancing across the pastel facades. Across the street, the two older brothers of the bicycle kid lifted weights shirtless in the front yard of the cracked row house. As far as I could tell, the three boys lived there alone, though they were frequently looked in on by a big-gone-soft man with a shaved head, a horseshoe mustache, and a ring of keys on his belt. His rusty Continental was a familiar sight around the neighborhood, as was his asbestos-faced sidekick with swollen eyes and a tireless body that he carried like armor. This strange and rugged creature had no name, and the neighborhood kids clamped quiet when the sound of his shopping cart with the screaming wheels rounded the corner, the block breathless as he pushed his battered buggy, crammed with pipes and hub caps and random hunks of metal, down the middle of the street. Vehicles would line up behind and proceed patiently in his wake. This man rarely looked at anyone and hardly ever said a word, though he would appear on occasion without his carriage, stomping down the sidewalk screaming up a riot. When this happened, the kids didn't only just keep quiet, they went inside.

It was back when I was gutting my house, filling a dumpster out front with loads of rotted lumber and crumbled plaster, that the bald-headed man had first approached me, his mule in tow. He told me that his name was Cyrus, and that *his man*— the silent one—would be working for me. I told him thanks, but that I didn't need any help. He told me again that his man would be working for me, and proceeded to tell me how much I would pay him. I told him again that I didn't need any help. They left. That night a monkey wrench crashed through my bay window and scraped across the parlor floor. By morning, it had been returned through the windshield of the rusty Continental. After that, neither Cyrus nor the silent man ever looked my way again, though the two weight lifting brothers would spit on the sidewalk whenever they passed by my house. And sometimes, in the soft pitch of night, I would hear the sound of the silent man's cart going back and forth in front of my house, until one of the neighbors would get up the nerve to yell out their window for him to stop all that racket.

On that particular Tuesday morning, I was smoking a cigarette and drinking coffee on my porch as the boys went through their daily weight lifting routine. They looked like convicts in a prison yard as they practiced angry stares and threatening poses. They stopped what they were doing when a skinny boy near their age rounded the corner, pumping the pedals of a shiny bike. A black doo-rag flew from his head like a pirate flag. He cranked past, did a loop in the street and glided away. The boys put on their shirts and followed him on foot. They did this every morning, whether school was in session or not. The youngest one, whose path I often crossed in the middle of the night, was not involved with his older brother's affairs. Or so it seemed.

I sat in the splash of the morning sun until the French girl bound down the blue-stone sidewalk, waving her arms and calling "*Nicoise! Nicoise!*" Her brown hair was tied back in a short pony tail and a red bandanna circled her neck; a sleeveless red t-shirt was tucked into blue-jeans cuffed up at the shin over sloppy canvas sneakers. Even in rockabilly clothes, she was sexy and adorable. Strolling through my gate, she smiled and pulled a cigarette from behind her ear, her big brown freckles blinking in the abundant sunlight.

"*Bonjour, Nicoise,*" she sang. Right up next to me on the top of the stoop, she sat. Our legs touched.

"And what are you so happy about?" I asked.

"Because, you have said to help me."

"Relax," I warned. "We're just having a talk here, that's all."

"Fine, fine, then," she said, flipping the cigarette into her mouth like a lollipop. "First I will talk. Then you will help."

I gave her a light. Smoke surrounded me. "Right," I said. "Just talk. And slowly, please."

"Okay," she said taking a deep breath, "I am from France, of course, but my brother, who is from France, too, of course, is artist, painter, and he go to the Art Institute here, on Brooklyn, and he is to call home every week, but when he does not call home for many, many weeks *ma mere*, my mother, she have worry so she call the school and they tell her he is not here the whole time and he has not made payment for the course, also, so she send me here, to, to find him, and I find his address, but he is not here, and I find the, how do you say, *concierge.*" She yanked her little dictionary from her back pocket and flipped through the pages. "Ah, landlord. I find the landlord and she let me into the flat, but I wait for many days but he does not come, and then one day he come and he find me there and he seems, um, *derangue...*" She went to her dictionary again. "Awful!" she said. "He seem awful..."

"All right," I said, but she continued on as if she hadn't heard me.

"...Ah, but it is not just how he look, but what he do. He, he," she made a pushing motion with her hands..."and he act crazy; he grab my bag and take my, *mon argent...*"

I held up a hand. "Money," I said, rubbing my fingers together. "Money."

"*Oui*, money," she said.

"Go to the police, then," I told her. "The precinct's only a few blocks away. I'll show you…"

"No!" she interrupted me with a smack to my thigh. "I go to the police. They are asshole. I tell them that he is not here, and they say, when do you see him, and I say last yesterday, and they say then he is not not here because you saw him yesterday, and I say but he is not here now, and they say, he has to be, to be away for some time, I can't remember for how much time, but some time before he is away enough for them to do something. At me, they laugh. They laugh."

I imagined that the cops at the local precinct must have had a field day with her. All the shootings and drug dealing and muggings and whatnot that went on in the neighborhood, and here comes this splinter of a French chic blabbing in broken English about a painter who looks bad and doesn't call home. I'm sure they were ready to drop everything to find him.

"The police are right," I said. "Someone has to be missing for a while before they're really missing. Even then, that someone's an adult here, a grown up. He can come and go as he pleases."

"Yes, maybe," she said, "but something is wrong, he does not look right, and he…" she did that thing with her hands, "and take my, my money."

"Did you tell the police that?"

"No! He is my brother. He is my brother and he is not here."

I stared out at the marble blue sky and thought about my dead brother Angie, and how much I missed him, and how he could never come back. If this girl was working me, and in some way I knew she was, she'd picked the perfect set up, as I was a sucker for a missing brother story.

\*\*

I found out that her name was Colette, and that her brother was Jean-Baptist Rennet, a painter—as if he could be anything else with that name. He was supposed to be registered at the art institute for the year, and was staying in a studio apartment on Myrtle Avenue. Colette had been staying at his apartment since she arrived from France. I went down with her to take a look.

Colette kept up her blab as we walked past the ninety-nine cent stores, fast food joints, bodegas and check-cashing places that lined Myrtle. Even in the sunny spring weather, everything seemed gray and sucked of life. Elderly men and women sat dumb in doorways on lawn chairs. Young ghetto girls, under-dressed and overweight, shuffled by, dragging children one could only hope weren't their own. Outside the methadone clinic, a huddle of junkies itched and milled and fussed with each other. An ambulance chaser handed out his cards as an ambulance sped by. Peddlers barked their wares of electronics and beauty and God. And around the edges and in the shadows, hostility gathered like the threat of rain on a cloud covered day.

Outside an apartment building on a corner, Colette fumbled for her keys. Inside a liquor store on the street level, an older woman read a paperback behind bullet-proof glass. A red-painted brick wall around the side held the mural of a little girl, her pig-tailed portrait above the years of her life: 1985-1990. "Stop The Violence" spanned above the industrial metal door where we stood. Colette thanked me for walking her home.

"That's it?" I asked. "No more looking?"

"I must go," she whimpered, looking under her bangs at the streets. "I don't want to stay here."

"All right," I said. "Let me come in for a minute."

"But why?" she asked.

"Take a look around. I don't know. See a picture of this person I'm supposed to find."

"He has no pictures," she insisted. "He has many, many pictures he makes, but he does not paint him."

"So what are we doing here then?"

"You take me home." She looked around with an expression of distaste and panic. A chrome-rimmed car cruised past, pumping beats through the speakers as a pack of teenagers cursed each other while crossing the street. Everything at that moment seemed to seethe, the air heavy from the exhaust of fast food joints.

"Okay," I agreed. "Go inside, but tell me what this guy I'm supposed to find looks like."

A flush of confidence swept her face. "He look kind of like me, we are close in years, but he look more like an artist, you know?" She traced her face with long fingers. "And no, no..."

"Freckles," I said.

"Yes," she sighed. "Not these. Freckles."

"Too bad," I said.

She smiled and turned her toe into the sidewalk.

"Anything else?" I asked.

"And his hair is messy and he does not eat so good."

"So," I said with feigned frustration. "I'm looking for a skinny guy with messed up hair and no freckles?"

Colette smiled and touched my arm. "Oh, and he usually has some hair on his face, here," she said, pinching my chin like it was a piece of fruit.

"What color?"

"I don't know, um, *brun*?"

"Brown?"

"Yes, brown," she said, curling a strand of my hair in her fingers. "But not *cho-co-lat* like yours." She offered a coy smile and went inside.

So I went off to find an artist with brown hair and some

growth on his chin, the word *cho-co-lat* echoing through my head.

**

The lady in the liquor store sold me a fifth of whiskey and the landlord's name and phone number without taking her eyes off the book she was reading. I went outside, and from the pay phone on the corner, dialed the number she had given me, hanging up when I heard the phone ringing back inside the liquor store. The woman closed her book and cackled as I returned.

"Damn, boy," she croaked. "Now don't you feel foolish, being all presumptuous and shit about an old black lady, thinking that there was no way I could own this building." She kept laughing, smacking her thigh and shaking her head. Her pulled back brown hair was streaked with gray, her dark skin shiny with moisturizing product. She lit a Virginia Slim and tapped it into a coffee can. "Now, what you want with Miss Lillian?"

"And how are you, ma'am?" I asked.

"Don't 'ma'am' me, boy," she warned.

"And don't 'boy' me, ma'am," I responded.

I put my fingers in my front pocket, and after a moment of staring, she slipped into a smile. "Well, all right then. We got ourselves a deal." She massaged her throat and spit into the coffee can. "Now what can Miss Lillian do for you?"

I asked her about the artist. She knew him. Said he'd been a quiet tenant and a regular customer since September. Came in every day for a bottle of wine, and always handed her his monthly rent check on time on the first, until he dropped from sight about two months back. She still had his deposit and hadn't moved on the eviction process before the girl with the freckles came in. She'd let her into the apartment a week ago in exchange for the back rent. The girl had asked her questions about cafes or such places, and she'd sent her up towards the heights. Miss Lillian knew nothing more than that. I thanked her kindly and made for the door.

"Might want to check that hippie school up the road," she yelled after me.

**

Below the billowing tree line west of the heights spread the Art Institute, a fence-rimmed fortress, two blocks by four blocks around. Inside the fortress were ancient industrial buildings and factories that had been converted into classrooms and dorms. A large, modern building was going up in the far corner. Within the metal bars lay a leafy quad. Shaded by the branches of plunging trees, students trudged on paths with their art supplies and coffee cups, bleary eyed in the noon sun. In their raggedy clothes, they looked like grown-up versions of the kids I'd grown up with. Since nearly every boy or man that passed by looked messy-haired and in need of a meal, I decided to step inside the campus in search of a French accent.

Just then a familiar face strolled by on the sidewalk, breezing along, laundered shirt blousing off his shoulders like the sails of a mast.

"And how are you, Will," I said.

He stopped as if interrupted from a dream and tipped his chin. He had an inch on me and a handsome brown face, his mustache and wavy hair trimmed and tight like he had just walked out of a salon.

"Oh, hey Stiles," he said. "What's up, guy?

"Not much," I said.

Will was a twenty-something man whose main occupation was buying old buildings in the neighborhood which he then renovated and flipped into co-op's or condos, whatever made him the most money. He lived in a carriage house just around the corner from The Notch, where he drank and bragged of his business conquests at the bar during my Saturday shift, and came, with a range of attractive women, to eat in the evenings.

"How's the spaghetti business?" he asked.

"Not bad," I said.

He laughed from his nose. "Not bad? Shit. I know it's better than that," he said. "The other night I had to wait an hour to sit down. Y'all need to learn how to move them tables over there."

The reason Will always waited so long for a table was because the Captain hated him, and usually waited a while before seating him. However, Will's ego was too big to register such a slight.

"Those are the rules," I informed him, trying to cover for the Captain's curious lack of courtesy. "Once you sit down, you can stay all night—that's the Captain's way."

"Yeah, well, that's just some stupid old-school shit right there," Will said, flattening his lips.

"Works for him," I said.

"Sure enough," Will nodded. "But does it work for you?"

"How's that?"

"Come on, man," he said, tilting his head like we were confidential. "I know you getting at least a cut of all that business you bringing in. That place was on the outs, only serving geezers, till you got there."

I told him I was happy to have a paycheck, and a place to spend my time. He laughed and smacked his palm with a cardboard cylinder.

"Art class?" I asked.

"Nah, nah," he laughed. "I have these future architects do my plans for credit, and then their professors certify them so they're solid with the city." He smiled like that was the most brilliant thing I'd ever heard. "Yes, sir, this school here is like gold."

"You don't say?"

Will's squinted and spoke without condescension. "This school's on the rise, Caesar. Endowment is way up. New dorms are being built. It's on the rise, all right, and with it will come the neighborhood. If the right people get involved in the future." He smacked the cylinder in his hand again.

"Got the future in there?" I asked.

"Yeah, got me a few new buildings, a little ways out." He gave me the address.

"That's my block," I said.

"No shit? That blocks coming up, you know. It'll be real nice someday."

"It's nice now," I said.

"Come on, Stiles. That block's ghetto. Good-looking ghetto, well-built ghetto, but ghetto all the same."

"You don't say?" I said.

"You got them hoodlum kids, half-a-dozen shells, that crazy-ass crack head around all the time. Does he live there or what?"

"I don't know where he lives," I said about the silent man, growing tired of this conversation, which reminded me of Saturdays when I was on the clock and obligated to listen to such chatter. I tucked my hands in my back pockets and watched the students pass by.

"Don't worry, guy," Will said. "I got one place ready to go once as I lose the last tenant, then a few more set to go soon enough. Yeah, I consider that block very important, and I'm about to get to work over there, and it will arrive. I promise you that. It will arrive. That's what you were hoping for when you bought the place, right, guy?"

What I was hoping for at the moment was that he'd stop calling me "guy."

"Not really," I said.

Will squinted again and lowered his eyes. "We'll then, the hell you want to live there for?" He chuckled at the end of the question.

I didn't really want to get into the whole family curse thing, and the promise to my mother to find a home, so I told him I'd always dreamed of living in a well-built ghetto.

"Shit, Stiles," he said, shaking his head with a laugh. "You a funny guy, a funny guy, and you gonna be a rich guy, too, once I get finished with that block." He pointed the cylinder at me to punctuate his pledge.

"And when's that going to be?" I asked.

"Good question," he said, air gushing from his nose. "It would be a lot sooner if I could find out who owns a bunch of them buildings. A lot of them crappy ones, the shells, even, are under the name of some corporation called Montclair, and they own a whole lot of property around here, a whole lot, but I can't find out who they are, so I can't buy them out. You didn't buy from them, did you?"

I told him that I bought my place from the family of a deceased matron who had lived in the house for all of her eighty-two years. Her kids had moved away and wanted nothing to do with Brooklyn anymore.

Will rubbed a broad shoulder and fought humility by tightening his lips. "I know people," he assured me, "so I was able to find their name and address from someone downtown, but it's just some cover and a P.O. Box. I send letters, regular, official and shit, offering top dollar, but they never respond. Shit, they even own that dump where them foster kids live."

"I thought that was Cyrus' house," I said, now interested in the conversation.

"Him?" Will laughed. "That fat fuck just a lackey for this

corporation, takes care of their property. That's all. Keeps them kids in there, and some other places, too, on a foster care scam."

"So ask him who he works for."

"You think I didn't do that?" he said, thrusting his neck and shoulders back. "Hell, I did ask him, with proper respect and everything, and you know what that mother fucker told me? To check myself before they found me in that canal where they dump the I-Talians. Can you believe that? Threatening a legitimate businessman. A brother, no less."

"So, how do you find out who he works for, this Montclair?"

"That's the million dollar question, Stiles," he said smiling and shaking his head. "The million dollar question. And I mean that, because once I find out and I can have me a sit down with them, they'll see that I'm legit and want to do some business. They just need to wake up, you know. Find out what time it is. Brooklyn's changing man, and you either get with it or get out the way."

"I'll find this company for you," I said. "I could use a million."

Will laughed and smacked the cylinder into his palm, "Now that would be worth something, maybe not a million, but something, yeah, man, for sure." He turned toward the open gate. "See you around, Stiles."

At the entrance stood a large security guard who looked like he had swallowed a smaller security guard. Sunlight reflected off his onyx head. Without being asked, obedient students formed a line before him and presented their ID's, which the guard studied before nodding them along.

Will walked right up, bypassing the line. "What up, brother?" he said and gave the big man a resounding handshake and a smack across the back.

"Not much, my man," the giant said with a down home

smile. "How you feel?"

"Can't complain," Will responded, his arms out to the side. "I have my health."

He passed through the open gate as the security guard shook his head and showed his teeth. His smile vanished when I tried to follow.

"ID?" he demanded.

I handed him a library card and he looked at me like I'd just served him half a sandwich.

"What if I'm with him?" I asked, pointing towards Will gliding through the speckled sunlight of the quad.

The security guard turned and barked, "Brother!"

Will stopped and turned around, a shaft of light splayed across his face.

"You vouch for this guy?" the security monster asked.

"He got ID?"

The shiny head shook sideways.

"Sorry," Will called to me, shrugging his shoulders. "Those are the rules, guy."

**

Half a block down, I hopped the fence and folded into campus, searching. The Registrar's office respected their student's confidentiality; the Bursar's office wanted my name. In the library, I read a detective story and peered around the room between passages. At the crossroads of the quad, I smoked cigarettes and asked every student that passed if they knew Jean Baptist Rennet. If the French kid went to school here, no one knew him.

A dreary girl came clomping along, black clad from neck to boots, rubber-soled and languid, like a contestant in a Tim Burton beauty contest. Hearing my inquiry, she deftly shifted direction without slowing her step. I watched. And when she looked back, ever so slightly, over her shoulder after a dozen yards, I trailed her towards the security gate and the behemoth guard.

"Catch you later," I said as I strode by the guard, not bothering to wait for his reaction.

Following the girl from the other side of the street, we walked in the direction from which I'd come. After a string of blocks with cracked sidewalks and public housing playgrounds, she crossed Myrtle Avenue against the light and slipped into a Mexican dive.

I followed her in. My eyes took a second to adjust to the dark room. I crossed the mottled floor and sat down at a counter that faced the kitchen next to two Mexicans who drank beer from bottles and didn't speak to each other. The room smelled of chorizo and eggs and warm tortillas. A ceiling fan turned the greasy air. The jukebox in the front corner was quiet and somewhere a customer ranted about some professor named Hamersley being a douche-bag and a sell-out.

A wonderfully fat waitress came around the counter holding a tray balanced with beer bottles and beveled shot glasses filled with gold liquid. Her dark hair led me to a booth along a putty-colored wall strung with chili-pepper lights. Four art-funky students crowded the table: three skinny dudes dressed-up like derelicts and the black clad girl whom I had followed.

After the waitress left, I stepped into the space she had vacated.

"And how are you?" I said to the girl.

She rolled her eyes again and looked away.

"I saw you over by campus before. Remember?"

"No," she answered with indifference, her eyes now on one of the boys across the table.

"Who the hell *are* you?" he asked me as if I was an unwanted admirer. He'd been the one bad-mouthing the professor. He wore a vintage t-shirt and a leather wrist band, and was small-to-medium-sized, even with his head held high and his hair in a junior brassy pompadour. The other two boys, who were both Asian, forked plates of runny food and hid behind their jet-black bangs. I kept my eyes on the girl.

"I'm looking for Jean-Baptist Rennet. You know him?"

"JB?" the one with the mouth asked. "What do you want with JB?"

"JB," I said to the girl. "You know him?"

"No."

"Who the hell are you?" the mouth demanded again, his voice rising.

To the girl I said, "I'm a friend of the family and they're worried about him. That's all. You know where he might be?"

"He doesn't have a family!" the guy cried. "He's from France, you ridiculous fuck!"

I pulled up a chair and flipped my smokes on the table. As the waitress passed, I ordered a beer. "His sister's here, at his place, but he's not around. Where's he been?"

The girl tilted her head down and said, "Get the fuck away from me."

I asked her again if she knew where Jean Baptiste was.

She licked her cracked lips and turned her face toward the wall. Her friend smacked his thighs and seethed at the ceiling. "Who the hell are you?" he demanded for the third time, pounding the table. The silverware shivered, but I didn't move.

I figured one more question would get me an answer; instead, it got me a tequila shot in the face. The girl's cackle, shrill and violent, stung my ears as I blinked through the burning liquid. Raw anger rang up inside of me, and I responded by scooping up the nearest knife and pinning it behind the big mouth's ear. I clamped the other side of his face in my grip. He went stiff and lost track of his breath. A hush fell from the ceiling. I smelled sweat. There was no sound except for the girl giggling into her chest. The waitress hurried my beer to the table and vanished. I held the knife against the boy's ear cartilage, testing it against his flesh, now calm enough to wish that I'd walked away.

"Listen," I said to her. "Tell me something, anything, about Jean-Baptist Rennet and I'll be gone."

A fly buzzed my ear. A fork hit the floor. The kitchen staff came out into the room.

The girl laughed and stared into my eyes.

"He's eight feet tall with purple teeth and three cocks."

Flesh trembled against my blade. I clenched the boy's ear with my thumb.

"Cut him," she dared. Her voice had gone husky.

I held her stare and waited.

"Cut him," she repeated, a hint of flirtation in her tone. "I want you to."

Her breath had picked up. I felt the boy quiver into the blade. He had a thin pink face and pork-chop sideburns; his blue-green eyes, now filled with tears, looked like swimming pools. I pulled away. "Professor Hamersley sent me," I said, spinning the blade close to his face. "Told me to tell you that your art sucks." The girl laughed up a riot, which followed me out the door.

Out on the avenue, with tequila in my eye and egg on my face, the brilliant sunlight made it hard to see. Still, I now knew this much: the Frenchman existed, so Colette was for real. However, I didn't feel relief. Based on the company he kept, the missing brother of Colette could be into something serious. Something I didn't need any small part of, but yet felt a great need to be part of.

\*\*

I walked back to the Art Institute and hopped the fence again. Activity on campus had paused for midday. Students sat on benches and under trees, eating lunch and smoking cigarettes. One of them directed me to the Visual Arts building, a red-bricked old factory with wide, arching windows and a dormant smoke stack. After reading the directory in the lobby, I scaled the wide stairs to the fourth floor in search of a name that I found stenciled on an open door.

The spacious office of Professor Reginald Hamersley was well-lit by natural light. On a washed-out brick wall hung a large portrait of a Latin woman in colorful clothes. There was no other art on display. I wondered how he got to his desk, in front of the window, through the minefield of sculptures and sketches and cylinders scattered on the floor. I coughed from the doorway, and an oval red face appeared from behind a pile of folders, tiny eyes glaring through small round frames.

"You must make an appointment to see me young man," he said before disappearing behind the folders. "You know the rules."

"I'm not a student," I said from the doorway.

The face reappeared, drawn and impatient. Wisps of white hair flitted above a balding pate. "Well, then, what do you want?" he asked empirically.

"I'm wondering if you know Jean-Baptiste Rennet?"

"I do," he said, bowing his head. "And why do you ask?" He had lost the arrogance in his tone, seeming genuinely curious about my presence.

I took a few steps into the room before bumping up against the ramparts of artistic expression.

"I'm a friend of his sister," I said. "She came to America to find him."

Professor Hamersley nodded knowingly. "Well, then, I'll tell you the same thing I told her."

"She was here?" I asked.

"No, she went to the dean's office last week. Caused quite a fuss, too, from what I understand. And they called me, since I am the department chair, and I told them that he had been essentially absent since school began last fall. He had registered and reported for classes, and then disappeared after a few weeks. I'm sorry I have nothing else to report. I really am."

His cordiality had me curious.

"But you remember him, from just a couple of weeks?"

Professor Reginald Hamersley cleared his throat and a splash of red flushed his jowls.

"Well, yes," he said. "Jean Baptiste Rennet was here on scholarship. His application portfolio was as impressive as any we'd ever considered. The fact that he was from the south of France only added to his appeal. It's not often that European artists, even young ones, come to the States to study. We were quite proud. It was a coup for the program, and so we had great hope for him, though now it's become a bit of an embarrassment."

"Sorry for your embarrassment," I said.

The professor squinted through his little glasses and pulled his tight mouth. Marching footsteps filled the hall behind me. Students conversed as they passed the doorway.

"Let me ask you something?" I said.

He nodded and stood up, a collection of portfolios in his arms.

"What makes him so good?"

"Fair question," the professor said. "Talent, of course, is subjective, though in the visual arts, the world of painters, especially, it is usually an ability to convey something, to capture something—an emotion or theme—that is subtle yet overriding, which differentiates their work." He pointed to the picture of the Latina on his wall. She sat with great posture and her chin held high. Sort of lovely, and sort of tortured. After a moment, the professor asked me what I saw most of all.

"Pain," I said.

"Very good," he said, getting up and walking carefully toward me with a respectful smile. He told me the painting was a self-portrait by Frida Kahlo, and, above all else, she knew pain. "Good luck with your search," the professor said on his way out the door. "We all hope you find him."

I looked at Frida Kahlo and her pain some more, wondering what made the work of Jean-Baptist Rennet so special.

Leaving campus, I bid Will's security guard friend goodbye for the second time that day. He cursed as I walked away.

**

The air outside was still, and the white light of a late afternoon burned into blue dusk as I entered The Notch. The Captain stood behind the bar, pouring Black Label for his friend Monroe, a gracious man as well as a handsome dresser: brown hat, crisp shirt tucked into creased slacks, pointy shoes polished to a high shine. He called himself the Captain's accountant, and he came in a few times a week for drinks, dinner, and a briefcase of receipts. They laughed about something as John Lee Hooker called "Boom, Boom, Boom, Boom," through the stereo.

"You're late!" Monroe snapped over his shoulder as I passed, his mustache flattened across an acorn-colored face. He smacked a hand on the bar and broke into a bright smile. "How you doing there, son?" he asked in a melodious tone.

"Fine, Mr. Monroe," I said, shaking his hand. "And how are you?"

"Better now," he said, rattling his drink.

The Captain chewed a wooden match and stared at me. "That French filly was in here before."

"And wha'd she say?" I asked.

"Hell if I know."

The two men cracked up.

"Wha'd you tell her?"

With a stare, the Captain questioned me for questioning him.

You think he told her, man?" Monroe interjected. "Fine little thing like that…he told her not to speak, just come back after closing, meet him by the back door."

The two men cracked up again. I started for the bar. The Captain broke from his fit to wave me over. "Hold on, hold on," he said, shaking out the last of his laugh. "She left this here for you." He slid a postcard across the bar. On one side was a colorful print of a four-story townhouse with a jagged city roof-line in the distance, a gigantic moon gleaming over a bridge in the background. Within the glow of the apartment windows were the silhouette of a cat, a piano, plants, and a small table with a bottle of wine and two glasses. I turned over the card and on the other side were an address and phone number for Jean Baptist Rennet, next to a black and white photo of the artist. He looked like his sister, minus the freckles and intrigue. His narrowed eyes spoke of affliction or affectation, maybe both.

The Captain snapped me from my thoughts. "You all right?" he asked, his fingers popping in my face. "Planet Brooklyn to Caesar!"

"Yeah," I said, pocketing the card. "I'm here."

"Good," the Captain said. "Start prepping the kitchen, I'll take care of the bar. I got a few more things to discuss with Mr. Monroe."

I looked at "the accountant." "Oh yeah," I said. "Tax season, isn't it?"

"*Sheeeeeeet*," the Captain drawled. "I'll pay my proper taxes to the government after I get my forty acres—they can keep their damn mule."

Monroe raised his glass and took a sip.

"Forty acres?" I asked the Captain. "And that'd be, what, the whole neighborhood?"

"Now you talking," Monroe said, nodding emphatically. "Now you talking."

The Captain studied me for a moment, then motioned with his head towards the back.

**

A pale light clothed the Captain as he drummed his fingers on a table by the front window, nursing a Cognac. He sat alone and stared out at the street. It had been a slow night, so the kitchen had closed early, though the bar stayed open. A single customer, at the far end of the bar, stroked the neck of a beer bottle and tilted his locks from side to side, considering Jacqui's bulbous backside. "Now that's a great big ass right there," he said as I started down the stairs.

Jacqui turned and squared her hands on the bar, her hair looping down in shiny curls. With a cocked head and mouth pinched to one side, her dead-serious eyes dared another word.

The customer, in work boots and construction clothes, passed a hand over the knotted beard that covered his dark face and neck. He nodded from Jacqui's swarming cleavage to her press-on lashes. "How you doing, darky?" he asked.

Her eyes held steady as her nostrils flared. She reached a hand under the bar, without shifting her stare, and searched around. I feared she was going for the bat we kept for security.

Instead she pulled a beer from the cooler and broke into a smile. "I'm doing fine," she said. "How you, Sweetie?"

"I-good," he said in a sing-song manner. "I-good."

I untied my bandanna and released the hair that stuck to my neck and shoulders. "You should get a new line," I suggested, sidling up to the man at the bar. "Might keep you from being part of batting practice."

"Nah, nah" he said without looking at me. "Don love everyone, and everyone love Don. Ain't that right, darky?"

Jacqui rolled her eyes and sucked down some beer.

"How about one of those for me," I asked her.

She gave me the look. "You got something for me, Mr. Man?"

I jerked a thumb towards the kitchen. She hustled upstairs, while I sat down next to my friend. Don was a one man construction crew. Before beginning the rebuilding of my house, I'd collected dozens of cards from dozens of construction specialists: sheet rockers, floor guys, plumbers, painters, electricians. Then Don showed up one day. I asked him what he did. "Ev-ry-ting," he sang. "Ev-ry-ting." And he was right. We worked side by side for nine months, and he knew more about houses than anyone I'd ever met. Even though his work for me was long done, he still showed up on occasion and without notice at the house or The Notch. We'd drink beers and talk about buildings and women. In many ways, he was my only friend.

"Hey," I said, nudging him. "You want something to eat?"

"Nah, nah," he waggled his fingers. "Took my vittles already. I just come by to see my partner, give he some numbers, in case you ever need me for nothing." He pulled up his jersey to display the phone on his belt.

"What a time to be alive," I said and finished off his beer.

He flashed two gold teeth and said, "Most definitely."

Jacqui came back from the kitchen and settled on a stool. She yanked the foil from her plate.

"What this?" she asked, her face hovering over the rising steam.

"It's a pork loin stuffed with garlic, fennel, and rosemary."

She took a bite and closed her eyes.

I went behind the bar, poured a glass of Chianti, swirled a ruby wave around the bulb and tucked it next to Jacqui's plate. "On the side is sweet potato Gnocchi."

She chomped a knuckle-sized orange dumpling, and swallowed some wine. Her face flushed with contentment. "Too bad I ain't into white boys," she said, poking her fork at me.

"You say that every night," I reminded her.

She shot me her look and returned to the food.

After popping two beers, I hopped on the back of the bar and lit a cigarette. I toasted to Don and took a big swig. The cold, bitter ale washed away the burnt sensation in the back of my throat.

"You have some paper?" Don asked me.

"What for?"

"*Jccht*," he hitched and rolled his eyes. "So I can give you my numbers!"

"Relax," I said, holding up a hand. Don was quick to anger, and slow to forget. He often talked about his childhood in Trinidad, saying he was "rough," and did "wicked *tings*," though I didn't know if he meant *rough* like he scraped his knees climbing mango trees, *rough* like a teenage derelict, or *rough* like the gangsters that shot each other up in those island films with reggae soundtracks.

Jacqui shrugged from her food when I asked if she had something to write on, so I patted my pockets and pulled out the postcard of Jean-Baptist Rennet. I clipped it to the cap of a pen and flipped it over the bar. Don scratched out his information then slid the card down the bar to Jacqui. "You can keep them numbers too," he said. "Case you ever need Don in the middle of the night or nothing."

She laughed and shot a sideways glance at the card. "Hey!" she cried. "I know this fool!"

"Who you calling fool?" Don demanded.

"Not *you* fool, this fool."

"What fool?" I asked.

"This fool right here!" With a red fingernail she poked the picture of Jean-Baptist.

"And how do you know him?" I asked.

"He came by the other night all sorts of messed up—you know, like the cat drug his ass in here or something."

"What night?" I asked.

"Thursday, I think."

"You sure?"

"Tell me the special."

"Fried tilapia."

"Oh yeah! No doubt about it, I was sitting right here eating that fish fry when he came in. It was about nine thirty. You'd just gone home, and the Captain was in back. He had me nervous, that one."

"Wha'd he want?" I asked.

"I don't even know," she insisted. "Like I said, he was messed up and shit, come up to the bar, started mumbling something with a crazy ass accent about coke."

"Wha'd you tell him?"

"What you think I told him?" she asked with a hostile face. "I told him this was a respectable place and he needed to take his narrow white ass out of here before the Captain come out and put a foot in it."

Don laughed.

"You know which way he went?" I asked her.

She poked her fork toward the door.

\*\*

Out on the street, Don and I walked in a slow-footed manner toward my house. "Good thinking going home," he said, tapping his temple with two fingers. "I have some smoke, fresh from the ground—no chemicals or nothing."

"You know I don't smoke that shit," I said, scanning the avenue. "Makes me paranoid."

"So why we leave then?" he demanded. "Them beer's was cold, and that lady like me."

By the time I finished telling Don the story of the French girl and the missing artist, we were in front of my place. I suggested he come with me to knock on the door of Cyrus's house across the street.

"No, no, no!" Don said. "They see me at the door and think I'm there to rob 'em or something villainous. You go, and I'll come along if you need me."

While Don lit a cigarette and waited on my porch, I angled across the street. The gate to the fence in front of Cyrus' house was missing like a busted-out tooth, and the path leading to the door was shifted and cracked. The open yard was overgrown, and littered with bottles and bags and the weights that the two older boys lifted. The front door was ajar, and I could see crumpled fast food bags strewn across the curling linoleum of the hallway floor. Voices and a pale gray light leaked through the ground floor window. I knocked on the door.

Blinds separated and then rattled closed. Footsteps approached until one of the kids, the middle one, stepped shirtless into the foyer and froze. He was stout and light-skinned with pimpled cheeks and hooded eyes. His hair had been picked into a globe-like Afro. He stuck his hands deep into his pockets and furrowed his face.

A voice called from the other room, "Yo, who is it, yo?"

Pimples, at the door, cocked his head to the side and yelled, "It's dat white boy from across the way."

"Fuck he want?"

"Hell if I know." Pimples looked and me and raised his chin. "Fuck you want?"

"A cup of sugar," I said. "I'm baking a cake and ran out, wondering if you could help me."

His face curdled up in confusion.

"You seen this guy around?" I held up the postcard.

"Fuck I know him from?"

"I don't know, but he's been around looking to get high and I thought maybe you might have come across him."

The oldest kid then rolled up in the doorway, chisel-faced and very dark with a high fade haircut. Shirtless, as well, he stood shingled off the shoulder of the boy in front. Both of them had the muscles and postures of grown men, but no sign of whiskers on their cheeks or chins.

"What?" Pimples asked, leaning forward, fake fury filling his already filled chest. "The fuck you talking 'bout, G? We ain't got no drugs round here." His breath smelled like pot smoke and onion rings.

"Damn," High Fade scowled. "What you think, just because we black we be selling shit?"

I leaned back and surveyed the block, then leaned in towards them a bit. "Let me ask you something," I said. "How many of the people live on this block are black?"

Pimples laughed. "All of them, 'cept you, nigger."

"That's right," I said, as they chuckled. "And you think I'm going door to door looking for this guy?"

They stopped laughing. I held up the postcard again. "He goes to the art school and has a French accent," I added.

They stared at me for a moment then looked at each other. Then High Fade smacked the postcard from my hand and backed into the foyer. Pimples slammed the door.

I picked up the card and crossed back over the junk-strewn yard, feeling electric and abandoned of my senses. When I reached the sidewalk, Don appeared like a fog in the night. "Oh, Caesar," he said, "you talking mighty fast to them gangsters."

"They're just kids," I said.

"No they not," he said. "Them most definitely not kids."

I went up the stairs and sat on my stoop.

"You sure you don't want any of this good smoke?" Don asked from the bottom of the stairs.

"Nah," I said.

"Okay then, partner, I'm going now, but you be careful with them gangsters, they shoot you where you stand."

I waved him away.

"All right, then, but if you need Don, you have his numbers."

He strolled down the middle of the street and disappeared into the night.

I lit a smoke and closed my eyes. The breeze picked up and brushed the hair off my neck. I remembered being a kid beside the tracks when a train whizzed by. Sorrow swarmed over me and spread through my cavity like dye.

A rustling by the gate opened my eyes.

"*Bonsoir, Nicoise,*" Colette whispered. "Something?" she asked. She had on a rumpled country skirt and a thin white top, ragged sandals by her side.

I shook my head and patted the stoop. She sat below me and leaned into my leg. Her dark hair dangled on my thigh. She held up two fingers in a lonesome manner. We smoked in silence, trading drags, our hands touching briefly each time. Energy shifted between us, but it was a sad energy, like we were waiting for things that we knew would never come.

I took the last puff, flicked the cigarette into the street, and motioned with my head toward the house.

**

Our footsteps echoed as we walked across my empty parlor toward the kitchen, leaving dirty prints behind on the hardwood floor. The kitchen was open, sparse and clean, with a single stool next to a large island. I had no table. From an overhead light above the island, white light spread on the granite counters and slate floors. Next to a basin sink, a stainless steel fridge hummed. The beech cupboards were empty except for bottles of wine, honey and sour mash whiskey. Colette sat on the island, her filthy feet dangling in the air.

"Break a strap?" I asked, taking the bottle of honey and a bottle of Chianti out of the pantry and placing them on the island.

"*Ouff,*" she shrugged, "I take them off. At home, in France, I live in the country, and it is not bad for me to walk with no shoes, so I think to try it here and maybe I feel more like home."

"And how'd that go?" I asked.

"No good," she said, sagging into herself, looking towards the blackened windows in back. Across the fence, a neighbor's security light glowed orange. Low music played from somewhere.

"Hungry?" I asked.

She widened her eyes. "Yes."

I went over and opened the fridge. Inside was a stick of salami, a bowl of mixed olives, a jar of Italian peppers, and a nice hunk of Gorgonzola wrapped in plastic. I pulled a baguette from the freezer, placed it in the oven, opened the bottle of wine and filled two glasses. Next to Colette's hip on the wooden island top, I sliced the salami and piled it with the peppers on a plate, the placed it beside the bowl of olives. We ate with our hands and washed the food down with wine. When we stopped for a breath, I refilled our glasses and removed the olive pits we'd left on the counter.

When the bread was warm, I took it out of the oven, sliced it in half length-wise, and spread the pungent Gorgonzola across the white loaves. Colette breathed through her nose and parted her lips. When she reached for a piece, I smacked her hand away. I then held the honey bottle high and let the golden liquid seep over the cheese. She moaned with her first bite.

We ate slowly, the honey blending with the strong cheese to create a salty and sweet sensation in our mouths. I refilled our wine glasses again and again, and we alternated slices and sips until the food and wine were gone.

As I relaxed on the stool, Colette brushed a strand of my hair to the side of my face. I took her long calf in my hand and lifted it to study her foot. I then went to the sink and returned with a warm washcloth and moved the stool between her legs. I wiped the soles of her feet and then the space between her toes, the top of her foot, her ankles and heel. She leaned back on her hands.

I then wiped her calves and the back of her knees. She tucked her skirt around her hips as I cleaned her lean thighs. Her breath increased, and when I arrived at her hips, she leaned back on her forearms, dunked her head and moaned at the ceiling. I peeled off her panties, and left them on the counter with the crumbs.

**

Colette slept alone on my mattress, covered in the milky moonlight spilling through the window. Beside the window, an extension ladder came down from the access hatch, allowing me to escape to the roof. Lying on a corroded chaise-lounge, I lit a cigarette and blew smoke at the velvet sky. A plastic bag, caught in the branches of a tree, fluttered like the wings of a bird. A jet soared overhead for a moment. A foghorn sounded in the Buttermilk Channel. The night was crisp and unforgiving as I smoked under the high moon, a dull headache pressed like a pillow tight to my senses. I'd recognized Colette's desperation tonight—it freighted her contact with me, and was returned to her in full. It was like something out of the past.

**

A year into my stay in Pittsburgh, another "niece" of Uncle, the man who owned the diner I worked in, arrived in America. She had shiny hair, skin the color of moon glow. Her name was Song. One day she walked up to my side and said "English." She wanted to learn the language, and I was the one at the diner who spoke it the best.

We spent most of our time in the library. We'd take walks when she needed a break, and she'd try her new words out on me as we cut through the Keystone winter, wind-whipped by the river hawk, Song wearing a down jacket with a fur-lined hood. One afternoon, on a city bridge, above the white-finned surface of the Ohio River, her face haloed by the hood and its ring of fur, she took my hand and said, "Kiss."

We spent the next several months stealing moments whenever and wherever we could: walk-in freezers, the dark and dripping basement, the customer bathrooms, in the filthy alley between overflowing dumpsters. Though someone was always home in the apartment upstairs her family shared with three other families, there was access to the roof via the fire escape in back. Late at night, when the weather grew warm, I'd slip into the alley and pull myself up the extension ladder to the metal landing, where I'd meet Song outside her window. Once up on the roof, we'd lay a tarp over the still-warm tar and be together under the Pennsylvania stars.

Song also played the violin. She would come to the kitchen at night in the middle of all the chaos, stand in the corner in a flannel nightgown and slippers, and play slow, flowing progressions in a melancholy key. Everybody listened, but I knew that the music was meant for me. For awhile, my fractured life seemed almost whole.

Towards the middle of summer, Song grew ill. She couldn't keep her food down, and her skin took on a pallid din. Uncle sent her away, with a promise that she'd return before her first school year in America started in September. Once she was gone, the kitchen grew tense, and I felt like I was being watched. Conversations ended when I approached, eyes avoided mine. My hours were cut.

One night Uncle announced that someone had been stealing food and that no one would get paid until the thief came forward. People at the restaurant stole food all the time, and Uncle had never said anything about it before, but this time he stormed around the kitchen, glaring into everyone's face. The immigrant staff was terrified, fearful of a fate much worse than anything Uncle could do to me. When he finally came to my face, his wrinkled, swollen eyes looked hard and long. I then knew why Song had been sent away.

I handed Uncle my apron and walked into the summer night of a city that would never be my home.

# *Wednesday*

I woke on the roof to the first blossoms of daylight. I was cold and covered in mist. The sun had yet to appear in the periwinkle sky, but the orange reflection on the rooftops promised another pristine day.

I shook the night from my bones and climbed down the ladder into my bedroom. I stared at the empty bed, hoping my morning eyes needed focus—there was no figure in the tangled comforter. I blinked and breathed. Then the stairs creaked.

Colette appeared atop the stairwell. "Al-low," she said softly, pulling at the ends of her hair.

"Hi," I said.

"*Je ne sais pas ou la toilette,*" she said.

"Downstairs," I said.

"*Je ne sais pas ou vous etiez,*" she said.

"Upstairs," I said, pointing towards the ladder.

She cupped an elbow in one hand and stared at the floor. Her arms looked long in my gray t-shirt, which hung on her like a nightgown. A naked knee cocked in, bearing weight. She lifted her tired head and searched the open room, which was the whole top floor of the house, a latticed-window on each side under the low ceiling. A mattress on the hardwood in back, bordered by clothes stored in milk-crates. Nothing more. I took her by the wrist and led her to the bed where we lay down together in the soft morning light.

**

I woke up a few hours later. The sun was bright in the window, and I could hear the sound of traffic in the street. Colette rolled over when I buttoned my jeans.

"Where do you go?" she asked.

"To look for your brother," I said.

"Oh, okay," she said. She sat up and shrugged, suspended between thoughts.

"You can stay," I said.

"Yes?"

"Yes."

She lay back down, and I covered her in heavy blankets.

\*\*

On the sidewalk outside my front gate were another pile of cigarette butts, smoked straight down to the filter. I looked up and down the block—no blue car, no strange people. I raised the hood on my sweatshirt and started down the street, until the silent man stormed the corner. "I'm sick of all ya' mother-fuckers!" he boomed. "That's right! Sick of all you mother fuckers around here. White, Korean, and Chinese! Don't come round here no more! Don't come round here no more. I'll kill all you mother fuckers and you're kids! Goddamn mother fuckers!"

These scenes happened about once a month or so, and in pretty much the same fashion, with him stomping around the block, ranting about outsiders and threatening their lives. It was usually just loud words, though, once, on a blistering August day, he took his pipe to the window of the Korean market around the corner. I'd been in there, alone by the coolers, grabbing some beers after a hard day of work on the house. The silent man had first passed the store in his rage, but then he doubled back to do a number on the storefront. The shattered glass covered the sidewalk on the outside and was halfway down the aisles on the inside.

As a result, I kept clear of him on his rage days. I darted

across the street and headed quickly to the Laundromat around the corner. In a hard plastic chair by the door, I fingered a local paper with an eye on the street. A TV blared with a game show as machines tumbled their loads. The room smelled of dry heat and chemicals. I put the paper down when the kid with the doo-rag came pumping past, his shiny bike glinting in the sun. A few moments later he came back the way he came, Cyrus' two boys rolling by after him on foot.

With my hood as a cover, I left the laundry and followed the three of them as they turned the corner onto a rundown block. Dandelions sprouted from cracks in the sidewalk. On the stoop of a shingled row house across the street, a sack of winos played the radio and sipped from brown bags. A feral cat hissed when I stepped near a tuna can tucked along a cyclone fence. Through the fence, in an open and littered lot, sunflowers turned their face toward the sky.

Doo-rag looped in figure eights as Cyrus' two boys leaned into the brick face of a building on the corner. I entered the shade of a bodega on the other side of the street. Samba music crackled from a radio on the counter, where a dingy man in a dingy shirt fed shredded meat to a tabby cat. The room smelled of roast pork and kitty litter. A sepia picture of Roberto Clemente was tacked to the wall. The dark aisles were empty except for a kid stacking drinks in the back. I bought a pack of cigarettes and stood on the small front stoop out front, next to a shirtless man asleep on a milk crate.

Leaning into a post, I smoked and watched the corner. A maroon Range Rover with tinted windows pulled up and all three boys huddled around the passenger side. The window went down and handshakes were exchanged. The window went up and the car pulled away. A few minutes later, a little boy on a little bike appeared. He stashed something in the side of a cement stoop and rode away. While the corner boys walked to the stoop of the brick building, I followed the little one who had made the delivery.

**

Gypsy cabs jockeyed and honked as I crossed Myrtle Avenue. Dollar vans lined the sidewalk and people piled in and out. As I walked down the slope, the buildings grew smaller and squalid. Trees vanished under the Brooklyn-Queens Expressway, and the heat picked up. Beyond the brick wall of the navy yard, the silver skyline of Manhattan glimmered in the distance like a mirage. The industrial remains of the flats were low and decrepit and mostly abandoned, though a few beeping forklifts unloaded trucks here and there. The storefronts were shuttered except for a bank busy with Orthodox Jews. The funk of a chicken processing plant contaminated the air.

I walked along the high brick wall that separated the navy yard from the street, frequently stepping over pulverized vials that sparkled like jewels on the sidewalk. There was no shade. I blinked away the dust. Across the street a one-eyed pit bull stopped and stared, baring its teeth at me until it caught a scent in the crevice of an abandoned factory.

"What up? What up?" a voice suddenly sang from behind me. "Looking for a pick-me-up this fine morning?"

It was the little kid on the little bike. The delivery boy. He had a round face and almond eyes that opened wide when meeting mine. "You Five-O?" he asked.

"Five-O?" I repeated. "What's that?"

"Five-O," he insisted. "PO-lease."

"Nah," I laughed. "I'm no pig."

"Who said anything about a pig?"

"When I was a kid we called the cops 'pigs,'" I said. "And

when they cruised by someone would sniff and say, 'I smell bacon'."

"You did?" His face lit up now. "Now that's funny."

The smile disappeared as he looked to his left and to his right. "So you want some rock or not?" he asked me when he was convinced that the coast was clear.

"That depends," I said. "How much is it?"

"Twenty dollars a tube," he said quickly, checking the scene again.

"Give me two, and I'll pay you twenty more if you let me ask you some questions."

"Questions? What kind of questions?" He set his feet on the bike pedals, ready to bolt.

"Don't worry," I said, pulling three twenties from my wallet. "A couple of questions and you're gone."

He squinted at me and pulled away. "You ain't into little boys, is you?"

"No, I prefer girls," I said. "All grown up."

"Okay then."

He took the money, slipped it into his front pocket and handed me the vials. Then he got off his bike and pushed it towards the cluster of brick towers staggered beyond the expressway.

"You live over there?" I asked.

"The projects? Yeah."

"What's it like?"

"I don't know," he said, eyes on the ground. "Noisy, and the hallways smell like piss, and people getting messed up a lot, but it's, you know, for the most part, just people living."

"And who do you live with?"

"My moms, but my grandmoms takes care of us because moms ain't really around."

"And where is she?"

"Out here," he said, brushing his chin over the bleak landscape. Figures began to move in some of the empty lots. A siren wailed out of sight.

"You ever see her?" I asked him.

"Once in a while," he said, "but usually just on the first of the month when the check come."

We walked past a soot-stained building with a stuffed dumpster out front. Rats were diving in and out of a hole they had burrowed through the metal.

"So your grandmother takes care of you and who else?"

"I got two sisters, they twins, Amanda and April. They in the fourth grade."

"And what grade are you in?"

"Sixth."

"Who's your teacher?"

"Miss Deborah."

"Nice?"

"Yeah, and smart, too. She make sure we do all our homework, and if we ain't in school, or even late, she calls up to find out why."

"You know Miss Angel?"

"Hell, yeah—everyone know her. I wish she was there when I was in the fourth grade. She Amanda's teacher though."

We stopped into the shadows under the expressway. The traffic rumbled by on the access road overhead. The girders were peeling paint. It smelled of human shit.

"How about this guy?" I asked, handing over the postcard of Jean-Baptist Rennet. "You know him?"

"He a teacher, too?"

"Nah, I thought maybe you might have seen him around the street."

"Nope," he said. "But I don't deal."

"Really?" I asked. "Then how'd we just meet?"

He pushed his bike across the street into the sunlight alongside a park. Acrid smells came from the men sleeping on the park benches.

"I'm a runner," he told me. "I run the shit back and forth between the projects and down here and up-a-ways, and sometimes something end up in my pocket, know what I'm saying? And I take it down in the morning, try and sell to the heads that up early."

He spoke with clipped clarity. I looked over his nice clothes and watch, his new leather sneakers.

"You should be careful," I warned.

"You don't have to worry about me. I keep it real low, and I do get paid, too, legit; mostly this other money I just give to my grandmoms."

"And does she know where it comes from?"

"Lookie, mister," he said, pressing up on his handlebars as we approached the projects. "She got a crack-head daughter smoking up the welfare checks and three grandkids to dress and feed—you think she give a hot fuck where the money come from?"

People came and went on the cement paths that fed the courtyard of the projects. The kid cleared his throat and got ready to peddle. "Look, I gots to go. You find out what you wanted to know?"

"Yeah," I said, handing him another twenty. "For your grandmother."

He smiled and raised his chin. "All right, then. Later."

"Hold up," I called. "What's your name?"

"Scottie," he said. "What's yours?"

I told him. He reared back and shot me a sideways glance.

"For real?"

"For real."

"That's cool," he said. "I like that. Well, see you around, Caesar."

"See you around, Scottie."

He pumped his little peddles and glided away, the sun gleaming off his chrome bicycle frame. I followed the flow to the avenue, left the locals at the bus stop and entered the park. I scaled the long rows of steps, then turned back to look over the little village of the projects. They seemed peaceful from this perspective. Past the rooftops, beyond the hidden river, the Twin Towers loomed in lower Manhattan like enormous middle fingers. I walked away with my hands clamped behind my head, elbows jutting out like wings, wishing the wind could carry me away.

**

Past the sloping green lawn of the park, I entered a new world, regal and historic. Here I walked on swept sidewalks, past pristine buildings and small shops and young mothers or West Indian nannies with children in tow on their way to the playground. Stylish women carried twine-handled shopping bags. The cafes were busy and a church bell praised noon as I ducked underground.

The walls of the subway platform were covered in graffiti and the advertisement posters had been disgraced. On the opposite platform, across a labyrinth of tracks and girders, a man in an orange safety vest swept up litter while whistling a tune. Below me, rats scurried between the rails amongst the garbage.

As I leaned against the tiles and waited for the train, a sense of unease began to rise within me. I knew that I should have taken this trip long ago, to face him, but now, at least, I had an excuse to go and see the orange man. It was time to find out if he was the one having me followed. At this point, I figured there was no connection between Colette and what I'd done at the beach.

I clutched the crack vials in my pocket as the train rumbled up and the doors opened and closed with a *bing* and a *bong*. Inside the car, an Asian man read an Asian newspaper. A young couple wrapped themselves around each other in the corner. A dented soda can clattered across the floor. The train lurched away and my stomach continued to burn. Fear crept up my throat and turned my mouth into powder. There was a pinching in my temples and a tension in my jaws.

The subway stormed through dark tunnels. After a few stops, the train rose above ground and daylight streaked across the walls and into the car. Below the elevated tracks lay Brooklyn: tree tops and roof tops, clustered neighborhoods like Allegheny towns. The water in the channel chopped and swirled around The Statue of Liberty. In the distance, the Verrazano Bridge stretched across the crystalline sky. Cars and trucks crawled along the raised expressway past the billboards and signs suspended in the open air. I sat with my head pressed against the glass and, when the shadows came, I looked at my reflection and wondered how I got myself in these situations, and if I would I ever get out of this one?

I got off at Coney Island, the very tip of Brooklyn, a neighborhood of amusement park rides and project towers. The rides were in motion, but the projects were still. Smoke rose from concession stands and the air smelled of sausage and shellfish. Seagulls circled overhead. The boardwalk bounced with teens on break teasing each other and flexing their energy. The oppressive white sun reflected off of everything, while the breeze carried the slight chill of the ocean. Beyond the empty beach, the gun-metal sea rippled with light. I sparked a cigarette against the wind and began to walk.

A little ways down the boardwalk, away from the carnival of Coney Island, a babushka in a bathing suit marked my arrival in Brighton Beach. I left the boardwalk and walked inward, past the stone apartment buildings where people read newspapers in open courtyards. Men playing chess raised their heads as I passed by.

On the main avenue, elevated train tracks towered over the street, bands of sun peeking through the breaks, making the light milky and surreal, like the images in an old film. People hurried along, speaking hard consonants with thick tongues. The street signs were in Russian and Yiddish, as were the storefronts, and the menus posted in the restaurant windows. The smell of cooking cabbage filled the air. Cars blew their horns as the train rattled overhead and soot sifted down like faint, dirty snow. Shifty types, vibrant with silence and danger, lurked in front of sign-less storefronts.

I turned a corner onto a residential street lined with attached houses of tasteless facades with small porches. Two Hasidic kids with black coats and dangling tendrils sat on the curb taking turns with a yo-yo. Dead center in the block, I walked through a low metal gate, climbed slate stairs and pressed the buzzer of a steel door painted to look like wood.

"Do you have an appointment?" a woman's voice asked through an unseen speaker.

I told her my name and that I did not, holding my face toward the hidden camera lens above the door. After a few seconds, the release of a heavy bolt sounded and the door opened to a vestibule and a large man with a shaved head and a blue tattoo of a spider web that covered his beefy face. An earring pulsed in his flailing nostrils as his eyes motioned for me to come in.

Once I was inside the dingy foyer, his meaty hands smacked at my bones. He took my knife, then motioned towards the back of the vestibule.

Through a red door, in a small white room, a woman dressed like a secretary with a pencil stabbed into her platinum bun sat behind a desk. "Hello," she said, lowering her head to look at me over her bifocals. "Welcome. Sit. He will see you soon." The woman at the desk changed all the time, along with the meat at the front door. The only constant was the orange man in the back, and, until recently, Martina upstairs.

"He will see you now," the secretary said a minute later. She sauntered to a door in back and held it open to a two-story room of vaulted ceilings, white brick walls and polished wooden floors. A wide, curving and carpeted staircase with a mahogany railing led to a balcony upstairs. The landing was lined with bedroom doors. In the back of the ground floor, deep red curtains rippled in front of floor-to-ceiling windows. There was a wet bar in the far corner. The air was cool and smelled of antiseptic and hair gel.

The orange man sat in the middle of the room on a large leather couch, his legs crossed, his arms spread wide. In front of him was a glass coffee table with a single folding chair on the opposite side. Reading glasses lay atop an open magazine. He wore khaki pants and a dress shirt opened enough to reveal the tip of a Jewish star hanging from a gold necklace. His sleeves were rolled up around scarred forearms, tight with rippling tendons. His plugged hairline was combed back off of a face dismantled by surgery and scars which always gave off an orange hue, hence my nickname for him (I didn't know his real name). His eyes were shattered gray with the blackness of a flame in the iris. I imagined him as a former spy or a gangster, maybe Israeli, but that was just a guess since I didn't know where he was from.

He motioned with his hawk nose towards the chair. "Caesar Stiles," he said with an undetectable accent and omniscient tone. "I'm surprised."

"And why's that?" I asked, hands flat on my thighs

"It's been a while."

"A few weeks," I said.

"More than a few weeks," he stated. "One month."

"Okay," I shrugged. "A month."

"Martina is not here," he said, locked on my eyes. "She's gone."

"Where?" I asked.

"I don't know," he said. "Maybe you know?"

"And how would I know?" I'd been lying all my life, often to some very dangerous people, but I knew if this mysterious and disfigured foreigner who spoke without an accent didn't believe what I had to say, I'd be dead by dinner time.

The orange man rubbed his throat and studied the lines on my face. A streak of sweat started in my neck and ran down my back. My heart felt like a little animal hiding in a warren from a deadly predator. No one scared me like the orange man. He seemed capable of unimaginable things, full of intelligence yet devoid of compassion, possessed of an unfathomable darkness which made me want to believe in God.

He finally spoke in a clipped cadence. "Your mother is dead. Your brother is dead. Your other brother is in jail. Your father's whereabouts are unknown."

I nodded.

"You have house in New Jersey," he said. "And it is empty."

I nodded.

"And you have house in Brooklyn. It is practically empty."

I nodded.

He licked his lips as an invitation to explain. Behind him,

the burgundy curtains snapped and billowed as if on command.

"You writing my life story?" I asked with a half smile.

His expression didn't change.

A mist of shame sprinkled my face. "I don't have much."

"You have two homes."

I blinked.

"But no life," he said.

The orange man then leaned forward and spoke slowly. "So that's why you helped the girl. She convinced you that she loved you. And, if you help her to get away, you can have a life together." His eyes and tone showed that he had seen this scenario before—his whores convincing their johns that they loved them, and that they could run away together. And that, of course, is what happened with me and Martina. Sort of.

I found Martina right after moving to Brooklyn. I watched her get out of a hired car and walk directly through a hotel lobby. I'd never seen someone so beautiful before, someone so sensual—and unattainable. The car she'd gotten out of parked in front of the hotel. I knocked on the window and spoke to the driver. He gave me a number and I arranged an in-call. I began to spend my Sundays with Martina at the house by the beach. I'd arrive after lunch, have a quick chat with the orange man, leave an envelope on the glass table, then go upstairs to one of the rooms off the balcony. Martina and I would talk a little, have some drinks and then fuck. I'd eventually doze off in her bed, and she'd wake me in the late afternoon to fuck some more. Then she'd give me a bath and send me home.

She was a kid, maybe twenty. Stunning—a true blond with the kind of legs that fall out of magazines, silver-dollar nipples and five thousand dollar tits. She could have made a mint modeling and even more dancing, but she was a prisoner of the orange man, she told me. He had brought her over from

Belarus on a broken promise of America—television and modeling, envelopes full of money to send home. Instead, he paid her next to nothing, despite the staggering amount he charged for her company, and threatened to kill her if she ever ran away. He also raped her on a regular basis. She told me she had family, second cousins, in Montreal, and with a little money she could get there and be free. If not, she swore, she would throw herself in front of a train.

I left her the money she needed one Sunday, and when I came back the following week, she was gone. The orange man told me she was sick. The next week he told me the same thing. I stopped coming after that. For awhile, I thought I was free of him, and her. Then the strange car appeared on my block, and the strange girl walked into the bar. I began thinking about the orange man again. I didn't want to run from him, and I couldn't live in fear of every new sight, like cigarette butts on the ground. I had no choice but to face him again. I decided to wait until he could help me.

I removed a crack vial from my pocket. "What do you know about this?"

He took it from me and held it up for inspection. The crystalline nuggets shone through the glass. He tossed it back to me with a look of disgust. "You want that shit? Go to the blacks."

"I took it off a friend," I said. "He's ruining his life over it, and I'm wondering why."

The orange man clasped his orange hands. "Drink?"

"Sure," I said. "Margarita, easy on the salt."

He got up, went over to the bar, and came back with two beveled glasses and a bottle of vodka that misted cold smoke. He filled the glasses and put one in front of me. I took a big sip that froze my throat and burned my chest. The orange man lifted a pack of Marlboro's from his breast pocket and opened the top in my direction. I took one and lit up. He did the same. Gusting air towards the high ceiling, I thought of the last cigarette routine in movies before someone gets killed.

"Feel that?" he asked. "That smoke, you feel it, right away, here," he said, touching his chest, then his forehead, then his shoulder. "Right?"

"Yeah," I said, aware of the way cigarettes slithered through the nervous system.

"It is because it comes in through the air, and that air goes everywhere, through your whole body and into the brain. That is why nicotine is such a good drug. You see?"

"Yeah," I said. "So is there something in there, like nicotine, that makes it so strong?"

"No," he said. "It is coke, weak, shit coke, cut with chemicals to make more. It isn't strong. If you take it through the nose, it doesn't work, really, but because you smoke it, it goes through body fast, and to brain, very fast."

"And because it's not strong," I said, "it leaves the body fast, and you want more, and because it's not expensive, it's not hard to get more."

He nodded and filled our glasses. "Perfect evil," he admitted with admiration.

After that, we drank silently for awhile in the sifting light. When I thought it was safe, I stood up to leave.

"Let me ask you something," I said. "Did you have someone follow me? In a blue car with Jersey plates?"

He cringed, as if insulted. "I could watch you sleep and you'd never know. Maybe I already have."

The Adam's apple bobbed in my throat and my heart fluttered like a small bird's.

"All that stuff about me," I managed to ask. "How did you know?"

His mouth hooked down at the corners. "Anything can be found out," he said. "If you know who to ask."

"If I asked you for the principal names in a corporation, could you find out?"

He nodded, a small smile curling up one side of his mouth.

I handed him the piece of paper with "Montclair" written on it. He put it in his shirt pocket as I turned to leave.

"Where are you going?" he asked.

"Home," I said, hoping the word would somehow transport me there.

The orange man held up a hand. "We have a new girl," he said with a nod towards the stairs. "Petra. She's Ukrainian."

"Same price?" I asked without pause.

"More," he said as his eyes turned to glass.

A snake twisted through my lower intestines as the blood dried in my veins. The orange man was suspicious of me, but not yet convinced. In the meantime, I'd have to satisfy him in a manner that he understood.

The stairs creaked as I climbed. I opened the door to what was Martina's room and stood in the threshold. There was a canopied bed in the center of the small room, an antique mirror, a bureau. Deep blue carpeting covered the floor. A redhead in black lingerie rocked in a chair by the open window, her foot over the sill, her toe, I imagined, dipped in the Black Sea.

"Come," she said.

I closed the door behind me.

**

On the subway coming back from the beach, I watched as the sun began to drop over the western sky. Thin clouds made a riot of pastels on the fading horizon. Pink light sparkled over copper rooftops and brightened brick facades. Planes left white trails in the thin blue sky. When the train dove underground, I laughed in the dark at my attempt at cheating someone like the orange man. He was a man I had no business trying to fool. A man I should have no business with at all. I checked my reflection in the subway's window and thought about what I'd become.

**

In Iowa, I had embraced violence and depravity. I worked in a shotgun bar full of losers, a ramshackle joint surrounded by cornfields on the outskirts of Ames. All day long I served beer in cans and liquor straight up to down on their luck men and their on-again, off-again girlfriends. They all had something wrong with them: addiction or physical disabilities or personality disorders, sometimes all three. The owner, a soulless old man into rackets, dealt pills and took bets, and many of the hapless who came to the bar to drink were in the hole to him. If they failed to fork over their drinking money, I was the one who had to take it from them. And this was never simple or easy because even the tamest scumbag will come up with some courage when their drinking funds are at stake.

As a result, I had to find a way to do my job with efficiency. So I went to the knife, as most people—drunk, disabled or otherwise—are frozen by the sight of a blade and the thought of being cut and the image of all that blood. I was thus able to keep the regular crowd honest for the most part, though on occasion, I'd still have to take a sickle-shaped nick out of someone's cheek. One dry evening, I even ventilated the game jersey of a degenerate linebacker from the state university. It was a rotten job, but I had nowhere else to go

I lived in the cab of an abandoned tractor trailer down the road from the bar. I slept in the storage space behind the seats and kept my things stacked on the dash. During the day, I'd run through the cornfields. With the shafts and loose husks tearing at my shoulders, I'd storm the open rows until my lungs began to seize. Then I'd take a drink of cool, cool water from a well before pumping rounds of push-ups off the rich soil. The smell of minerals filled my nose as my chest and back tightened.

In the late afternoon, following my workout, I'd sit on the tin roof of the bar, smoke cigarettes and watch the rows of corn swim in the wind. Crows flapped through the steady air to rest on black wires and consider me. In the distance, tractor dust billowed from above a river that wended through a field sewn with heather. Enormous cloud formations, like white buffalo, roamed the great plains of the sky, floating giant pools of shadow on the vast flat lands. And there on the tin roof, the Iowa sunset in my eyes, I'd think of my abandoned mother and my dead brother and my missing father and wonder if there would ever be a time when I wouldn't feel so alone.

The wife of the bar owner was a strawberry blond who wore cowboy boots and rodeo skirts. She was easily twenty years older than me, though her age was only evident in the skin that gathered around her elbows and the lines that webbed her eyes when she smiled. She was sweet and moody like a child, and even made faces like a little girl.

Most nights, she'd saunter in around closing time, her colored skirts swinging through the muted light of the bleary room. She would sit on a stool at the end of the bar, smoke my cigarettes and sing sad songs. While I tossed the late night lingerers, she'd take a fifth of whiskey in back, not returning until the bottle was empty.

With her husband passed out in his chair, his feet on his desk and an antique pistol across his lap, she'd take me by the hand over to the pool table, where she would peel off my clothes and wash my drawn skin with a warmed up bar towel. Then, with her childlike voice and sweet blinking eyes, she'd ask me to do things I'd never imagined. No matter what we did, how deranged or complicated or possibly illegal, she always kept her boots on.

Towards morning, in the cresting orange dawn, on the hood of her car in the parking lot, she'd braid my hair and ask me how the previous night's sales of booze and pills and bets had gone, telling me that part of the take was mine, due to the work I did for her husband beyond fixing drinks. Her math was a mystery, but her reasoning seemed right, so as the sun rose on the honest earth and its honest people, I'd hand my mistress the money and pills I'd stolen from her husband. She said she'd keep it for a rainy day.

One stormy night, amidst the hailstorms of August, the bar owner stumbled from the back in a stupor, the pellet-rattle on the tin roof having roused him from his bourbon dreams. He came into the barroom rubbing his eyes, opened them, and saw me standing there naked next to his wife, who was on the pool table with a long-necked bottle of Galeano stuck in her ass. He held up his and hand, then walked back into the office.

He returned a moment later, firing his old revolver with a shaky hand. His wife and I hustled off the pool table, the bottle of Galeano smashing to the floor, leaking its syrupy liquid. As bullets ricocheted around the room, blasting the lamp above the pool table and throwing green glass everywhere, we scooped up our clothes and ran out the door, both of us naked except for her cowboy boots that clacked across the wooden floor. The last thing I heard was the old man cursing as he slipped in the spilled liquor and squeezed one last round through the mirror behind the bar.

We tore through the frozen rain into her Volkswagen. With the keys already in the ignition, she started the car and spun gravel through the length of the parking lot until we fishtailed onto the rural road. We were still naked, hail and glass falling from our hair as the car split the fields, headlights on the frozen rain that exploded off the hood like popped corn. We drove dead west in total silence. Eventually, I passed out.

When I woke it was bright daylight, and we were sixty miles from Denver. She checked us into a motel on a ridge above a truck stop. The air was warm and bright, the mountains in the distance topped by snow. Her trunk was full of cash and pills, and we spent the next few weeks dealing amphetamines out of our room. When we weren't dealing we sat by the hotel pool, drinking champagne from plastic glasses, or had sex, without stunts or gadgets.

She told me we'd be leaving for northern California soon, where we'd live on grapes and love in the hills and hollows of wine country. But first, before we left, she had to tell me about her motherless childhood, about being the daughter of a two-bit rodeo owner from Colorado, and about how we were only a few miles from a home she hadn't seen since she was seventeen. She told me how she had grown up as a rodeo princess, adored by the crowds who came to see her, but ignored by her father, a man who viewed the world through the lens of profit and performance. She may have been heralded in public, but after the dust had settled and the crowds had gone home, she was invisible.

She told me how, when she came of age and became a beauty, she first flirted with and then fucked every hired hand she could coax into the barn, just to get her father's attention. He paid her no mind—until the day he caught her in the hay riding a midget rodeo clown named Little Willie. Her father lashed her into a pulp, then sent her limping into adulthood on her own. Since then, she'd been married four times, failing, again and again and again and again, to find a kind of love she had never known. In the pale light of the motel room, in the tangled sheets of our bed, I'd finger the whip marks on her hip as she hummed a sad song. Each drunken night we'd talk about California, and then in the morning, I'd wonder if we would ever get there.

One afternoon we returned from the pool, bursting through the door with her legs around my torso and a sunburned nipple in my mouth, into the presence of a dusty man with a drooping mustache sitting across our bed in a wrinkled shirt and jeans. He chewed on a match and squinted against the flood of light; uncrossed his boots and put them on the floor, shook the dust from his bones. "Get dressed, Belinda," he finally said with a craggy voice. She stomped a foot, pouted for a bit, then did what she was told.

The mustached man pulled a revolver from his shoulder strap and pointed the barrel dead-center at my chest. "I'm supposed to kill you," he said, twitching the barrel and staring at me with lazy eyes. When the girl was ready, he waved me aside and led her through the doorway and out to his pick-up truck. She offered no resistance. He threw her bags in the flatbed, hitched the Volkswagen to his tow, and climbed inside the cab. She waved to me out the window as they drove off together into the yellow afternoon. I stood in the doorway, blinking away the blindness and fighting my return to the world of sorrow and loss.

That evening, I bribed a trucker with a bag of pills and we chomped black beauties and barreled through the western night, up and over mountain passes bathed in ghostly light, down through canyons as bare and blasted as the face of the moon. As the sun rose on the desert, we killed everything in sight, leaving jackrabbits and snakes and armadillos flattened in our wake. By the time we reached Texas, I had forgotten all about the sad rodeo girl.

**

I climbed from the subway into the remnants of the early evening spring daylight. About a block from the station I spotted Angel staring down four large boys who formed a semi-circle around her. Two of the boys were standing, while the other two were slouched over bicycle seats.

"No, you listen to me," she said, lecturing like a teacher on her last ounce of patience, her hand balled into a fist tightly buckled on her hip. "I don't care if you didn't mean nothin' by it. If you want to greet me when I'm passing, you do it with respect. I'm tired of y'all thinking it's appropriate to talk to a woman like that. You all should know this by now."

I walked from behind her, my hands deep in my pockets. When the boys saw me, the expressions on their faces shifted from boredom to disgust. They sucked their teeth and rolled their eyes; two of them spat on the ground. It was then that I recognized three of them—Pimples, High Fade and Doo-rag. I didn't know the forth boy. Over their shoulder, on the far corner across the street, I could see the little boy who rode around at night straddling the frame of his bike and watching the whole scene with wide eyes.

I asked Angel if she were all right.

"Oh, hey Caesar," she said with forced casualness. "How are you?" She gave me with a poised smile, but her fists were still clenched.

I asked, again, if she were all right.

"Oh, I'm fine," she said, "I was just having a conversation with these young men." She waved them away with a flick of her wrist.

"*Boo-jee* bitch," Pimples said before signaling the others along. They scattered across the street, stopping a car that had the light.

"Wha'd he call you?" I asked Angel.

She puckered her mouth and shifted her hips. "He called me *boo-jee*, short for bourgeois, which, according to them, I must be because, because...." She shook her head and failed to finish her explanation. "I'm tired of this, you know that?"

"Tired of what?"

"Nothing," she said. "Nothing. Are you going home, Caesar?"

"Yeah," I said, holding out my arm. "Come on."

She took my elbow with a shaky hand. The trees that lined the streets, holding what was left of the spring fruit blossoms, looked like giant bouquets stuck in the sidewalk. A breeze picked up and showered us in white petals as we walked home together in silence, her fingertips on my forearm, her hips switching at my sides, our eyes straight ahead. The weight of her arm made my breath shallow. I thought about the day she had come to see the apartment.

Wearing a terry cloth sweat suit, she hopped out of the passenger side of a shining Pontiac with Maryland plates. An oversized man with a horseshoe of hair around the side of his head got out of the driver's side and lumbered up to me. He gave me a meaty handshake and introduced himself rather seriously as "her father." Even though the open house I had advertised had been over for half an hour, producing no less than three solid tenant possibilities, I still agreed to show them the apartment.

It was a one bedroom on the street side with an open kitchen and living room in back that allowed in light. During the tour, Angel pointed out all the things she loved about the place to "Daddy"—the built-ins and pocket doors, restored details and working fireplace. At one point, she looked out the wide back window and asked me about the garden. I asked her for a deposit and she smiled.

Before cutting me a check, "Daddy" asked me a whole lot of questions, studying me with suspicion the whole time. Eventually, I had to show him the deed to prove I was the rightful owner of the house. He apologized and said it seemed strange for such a young man to own such a fine house. I told him it wasn't so fine when I bought it. We signed the lease, and a week later I helped him move his daughter in.

Angel and I weren't much closer now than we had been on moving day. She slipped her checks under my door every month, and beyond that, we rarely had any contact. When we did run into one other, she treated me with polite detachment— a few words in passing, nothing more. As we walked home, her hand inside my elbow, I wanted to ask her about Easter, about anything, but I was silenced by her tense grip and faraway stare. There was also someone, I hoped, still upstairs in my bedroom. So, when got home, I left Angel at her front door and turned to head upstairs to check on Colette before reporting to work. I didn't even make it to the front steps.

**

A cigarette hit the sidewalk, sparked and settled amongst the pile of filters, then died under the steel-toe of my brother's big boot.

"What do you say, C?" he asked.

"Not too much, Sallie."

He laughed to himself. "That's it? That's all you gotta say— not too much, Sallie—after, what, how many fucking years?"

"Don't know," I said.

He'd grown older since I'd seen him last, and his voice had gone rough from cigarettes, but, otherwise, he seemed the same—jeans, boots and leather; cigarettes and fury. Except for bigger shoulders and a neck with more veins, prison hadn't changed him.

Sallie flared his nostrils, twisted his neck and considered the block. "You're not an easy guy to find, you know that, C?" He lit another cigarette and jetted smoke through his nose. "I had to pay a fucking detective."

"Blue car?" I asked.

"What?"

"He drive a blue car? Chrysler with banged up fenders?"

"Yeah, that's him," he said. "And he charged me a thousand fucking dollars to find your ass."

A woman from the block hurried down the sidewalk past us, two small children in tow. My brother squeezed the wrought iron fence in front of my building. Smoke drifted into his eyes, but he didn't blink. "Let me tell you something, C," he said loudly, "you want to live with the spooks, you could'a come to the can, saved yourself some coin."

The women dragged her children across the street and crucified me with her stare.

"And what do you need, Sallie?"

He laughed, a thick, guttural sound. "The fuck you think I need?"

"A library card?"

He smiled for a second. Then his face went flat.

"You're a cunt. You know that, C? A smart mouthed fucking cunt with faggot hair and a faggot mouth." He stabbed his cigarette at me as he spoke. "You talk like dad, you know that?"

"And how's that?"

"Like that," he said, pointing again with his cigarette. "All that bullshit sounding bullshit. You always loved that shit, you little faggot. Fucking prick always following him around, listening to his bullshit." He snorted with disgust. "You know why he left, don't cha?"

"Cause he couldn't stand the sight of you."

"No, fucker, I woke him up one night with a .45 down his throat. Told him if he didn't get his ass out of town I'd end him."

"That was nice of you," I said in the distant manner I always used to deal with Sallie, though heat lightening flashed in my sternum at his mention of what he claimed to do to our father. I never stopped wondering why he disappeared like he did.

"You were smart to run away, too, 'cause I'd a killed you," Sallie said. "I'd a killed you for what you did to Angie."

"Fuck off," I said, my pores open and jetting sweat. "I didn't do shit."

"You were there," he said, sucking smoke and smiling. "That I fucking know. And don't think for a second that I bought all that bullshit you told the police and Ma."

He seemed so sure of himself, standing in the street in front of my house, staring at me. I recognized his baleful glare, the arrogant twist to his lips, the eyes absent of compassion. While we were technically related by blood, we had never been brothers. Growing up, he was nothing more than a danger I had to avoid. Once we were separated, he never crossed my mind or entered my dreams—I had no idea that he'd been the one looking for me—but now here he was, telling me, with words freighted beyond his comprehension, that he'd run off my father and that I was to blame for the death of my brother, the two saddest events of my childhood.

"You paid a thousand dollars to tell me that?" I asked.

"No," he said. "I'm here for Ma's house."

"Ma's house isn't here."

"No shit, fuck nuts, but I went there and it's all boarded up. I knew she was dead, they sent a guard to tell me that, but I figured we still lived there 'cause no one told me nothing about it being sold. You know?"

"You into figuring now?"

"Yeah, I am, and the way I figure it, you took some of her money to live here, for whatever fucking reason, and that makes Ma's house mine. Fifty-fifty. Even Steven. Know what I'm saying?"

"It's not Ma's house anymore, it's my house."

"Says who?"

"Ma's will, my lawyer, the town I pay taxes to, that's who."

He laughed a little. "None of that means shit to me and you fucking know it." He lit a cigarette off the old one, flashed a twisted smile. "That's a foxy black chick you got there," he said, squeezing his cock through his jeans and nodding towards Angel's door. "You pay for that shit or does it come with the rent?"

A livery cab pulled up down the block and a family got out with their groceries. A man passed by walking a yellow dog. The youngest boy from across the street watched from his porch as pigeons flipped overhead. Sunlight graced the quiet street. The voices of children carried down the block on a breeze that nosed around my neck, cooling my skin ever so slightly.

"Let me see some people," I said to my brother. "Come back Saturday, about this time."

"Smart move, C," he said. "Smart fucking move."

**

I forgot about Colette and headed straight to work in the dying light, walking fast and thinking furiously. After about a block, my rushing thoughts were interrupted by a clacking sound coming from behind me. When I turned around, I saw the boy from across the street half a block back, the clacking coming from the card pressed against the spinning spokes of his bicycle tire. He weaved between cars, obviously trying to avoid being spotted. It felt like I was being followed by a lost puppy, and I was in no mood for puppies at that moment, even a sad and lonely one like him.

I turned the next corner onto DeKalb Avenue and waited against the wall of a coffee shop for him to pass. When the sound of his wheels got close, I stepped in front of him and grabbed his bike by the handlebars. His eyes bulged behind oversized glasses as he reared back. He reeked of body odor.

"And what do you want?" I asked without curiosity.

He tried to speak, but the words fumbled off his crooked lips.

"How's that?" I said, shaking the bike a little, twisting the handlebars in the process.

"N, n, noth," he said. "I d-don't want nothin'."

He looked off down the street as his nose began to run. People began to stop and stare. Cars slowed. From across the street, a woman's stern voice asked just what I thought I was doing. I let go of the handlebars.

"We must have been going in the same direction," I said calmly. "My mistake then." I tried to pat him on the shoulder, but he pulled away violently and peddled down the block. A safe distance away, he wheeled around. Without stuttering, he yelled in a taunting tone, "I've know that guy you looking for. That one who talk funny. He around. He around. And he messed up. Bad."

"Come here," I called with a conciliatory hand in the air. But when I stepped in his direction, the boy gave me the middle-finger and thrashed off on his bike.

\*\*

I gave myself the night off from work and took a city bus along the waterfront, past the active piers and warehouses, to the last stop. From there, I walked across a massive range of public housing buildings, like an endless reservation with outposts staked into the land. Many of the residents took notice of me, a white boy with long hair walking through the projects. Conversations ended or began as I passed. I pressed through the heat of hard stares and fought the discomfort of being unwanted and possibly in danger. At one point, a bottle broke behind me. At a corner by a playground, I passed a group of girls who were jumping rope. One of them, in a halter top, short-shorts and high-top sneakers, broke into a dance of pumping limbs and thrusting hips that nearly knocked me across the sidewalk. The girls laughed themselves silly over that.

Past the projects, the land opened up and water came into view. The breeze carried rain and salt. Jetties and barrier walls supported the shore, which was stacked with crumbling brick warehouses. Out in the channel, the Statue of Liberty stood alone on her little island, her corroding flame held high in the air as the sun set over the industrial shoreline and skyways of New Jersey. Across the narrows, the bluffs of Staten Island wavered in the smoky light of dusk that turned the Verrazano into bronze. Faint light burnished water busy with freighters and tug boats. A lone sail boat flitted in the distance. On the near shore, on a slip of water between a jetty and the land, a blood red barge bobbed on the tide.

The land before me was vacant except for kids playing soccer in a dusty lot. A cloud accompanied the scrum surrounding the ball. A small group watched from alongside a fence. After noticing me, two motor bikes started off towards the barge, while someone on roller skates launched in the opposite direction. The person on skates disappeared for a moment, before suddenly gliding by me, his hands behind his back. He did slow, wide circles around me as I kept walking on the cobblestone streets.

The wind stung my eyes as I got closer to the barge, where the two mopeds were angled like a spearhead. In front of the bikes, two boys stood, concealing something by their sides. The soccer game had stopped, and all the players were now holding bats and pipes.

"You have a reason?" the kid on the roller skates asked as he glided backwards well ahead of my steps, his wheels clicking on the cobblestone. He wore faded denim overalls with no shirt underneath. His thin muscles rippled and shined.

"I'm looking for Don," I said.

"What for?"

"Wanted to see if he could come out and play."

He held up his hand and stopped rolling, drew a line with his eyes on the ground. He pulled a hand held device from his back pocket and looked me over while he whispered into it. Darkness came fast to the open land and sky. The night dropped and a rat ran across my boot. It scurried to a wharf that vibrated below screaming seagulls. A fiery moon appeared above the bridge.

Having heard the communication, the roller boy rolled his eyes, sucked his teeth, and relaxed. "What island is King of the Caribbean?" he asked me.

"Tobago," I answered without pause.

He laughed through his nose, spoke into the device again, then waved me along. I noticed the pistols at the boys' sides as I split the motor bikes and crossed a landing to the barge. The dock creaked under my feet as the black water roiled below. I stepped through the opening of the barge to find Don in a soccer jersey and shorts, sitting across the open room in a grand wicker chair. A ceiling fan turned overhead and shifted the knit stack that held his hair. The walls and floors were made of wide wood planks, lacquered to a high shine. The furniture, all wooden, had been crafted by a master. I sat on a bench built into the wall, lined with white cushions. Parakeets chirped from a covered cage as the waves lapping against the belly of the barge.

"I like your house," I said to Don. "Very traditional."

"How'd you know where I stay?" His tone was playful, yet suspicious.

"You told me once that you take the bus till it stops and walk to the water."

Don rubbed his chest. "How come you don't use my numbers? It not so safe out there, you know?"

"Seems safe to me," I laughed. "Might be the safest place in this city."

He offered me a beer. I held up my hand when he started to stand, then got up myself and walked around the darkened island overhung with pots and pans. Around the corner in an open doorway was a black girl with white teeth and goldfish eyes. She leaned into the jamb, smelling of sweet oil. Her canary camisole glowed in the moonlight that came through the porthole behind her. An unmade bed filled the center of the room.

"Hello there, sir," she said in a sing song voice.

"And how are you?" I asked.

She blinked and blushed. "Fine."

"Get back in the room, Safia," Don called out.

She waved goodbye and closed the door.

The kitchen smelled of eastern fragrance. The refrigerator was stocked with foreign foods and beer. I brought two bottles back to the sitting area, took my spot on the bench and told Don I needed a gun. He puckered his lips and popped the top of his beer.

"How come you asking for a gun?"

"I might need one soon," I said.

"It's them gangsters across the street, right?" he asked. "I told you about them."

"No," I said. "It's not them."

"What then," he asked. "You want to take up pigeon hunting or some shit?"

"Nah," I said. "A different kind of hunting," I said.

He sipped his beer and looked away. "What you have to hunt?"

"It's a long story," I said. The floor began to sway from the water underneath.

"Every story long, Caesar, but they get short when the gun comes out. Quick-quick."

"What if I told you I didn't need any bullets?"

The barge bobbed and the stirred breeze tangled my hair. Don stood up, crossed the room and pulled open a trap door, disappearing into the floor. A few moments later, he returned from below with a charcoal-colored pistol pointed toward the ground.

"No bullets?" Don asked.

I nodded.

He popped out the clip and sent the bullet from the shaft into the air. He caught it and flashed his gold teeth. He handed me the gun, and I tucked it into the front pocket of my sweatshirt and reached for my wallet.

"No, no," Don said. "The gun is free. It's the bullets I'd charge you plenty for."

Under the sway of the tide, we sipped the rest of our beers in silence. When we were working together on my house, we'd often go days without talking, until Don would suddenly start speaking out of the blue, and not stop for hours.

"Why you come see me for a gun?" he asked. It had grown dark inside the barge and all I could make out was the outline of the chair and Don's high head dress. I didn't answer.

"When I was growing up in Port of Spain, I did wicked

*'tings.* I ran with older cousins and they friends, and we made plenty of trouble. I didn't mean no harm nor nothing, but we did enough bad things that my mother, she send me to New York when I was thirteen, to live with an uncle. Mr. Brown was he name and he had an electrical shop on Myrtle Avenue. I didn't go to school. I worked for he and learned he trade. Then he sent me to work for someone he know that a plumber. When I learned that, I start working with a painter. And it like that until I learn everything. Mr. Brown tell me, in America, if you have a trade you can always work, and he right, they always building and working here. So after I get my papers, I go out on my own. I work every day and sent money home so my mother could dress my brothers better, send them to school with proper things, keep them away from troubles."

He sucked his teeth and finished his beer. "No problem," he continued, "until ten year ago or so, when all these drug come 'round. Then the street out by Mr. Brown full of these little men selling they poison everywhere. They stand right in front of Mr. Brown's shop. They show him no respect. A grown man asked children to move on, to stop breaking laws and they curse he out like he nobody. So Mr. Brown set up a camera and make a tape. He capture everything. All the things on the block. The set-up and delivery and everything. He take it to the police and they come down and make some arrest. The next day the people them kids work for come round looking for Mr. Brown. Someone at the police tip them off or something. They shoot out the windows and set a fire in he shop. They might know Mr. Brown live upstairs, or maybe they don't; either way, he die from the smoke."

We sat quietly in the wake of that sad story until Don shifted his body and began to speak again.

"I find all this out from a guy I sometime do work for. He

asks if I know the Trinidadian man out on Myrtle who had he store burnt down. No news or nothing. No phone call from the police. A man die and nobody do nothing. They had he just sitting in the morgue. I took Mr. Brown back to Trinidad and laid him down in the proper ground. Then I come back to New York to clean up his shop, save some of his things, maybe fix it up, and I find them same boys back out front.

I lay low for a while. I mind my own and make a plan. What I did back in Trinidad when I was little was rob people. I never hurt nobody, but I robbed them good. My cousins and them, they taught me how it work and it was easy if you knew what you was doing. It like fixing up a house or something—it easy if you know what you doing. And so I watched them little devils and I found out who they work for, and who *they* work for. And one night, when the money moving, I walk right up on them in the proper spot and take it all off they hands. No problem. I have a white nylon panty hose over my face and I tell them that the ghost of Mr. Brown just been by and that he be back regular until they fix up that shop."

"They fix it?" I asked, the sudden sound of my voice unfamiliar in the dark, hollow room.

Don laughed. "Sure they do. They fix it up good. And then I sell it and send the money back home."

"Good for you," I said, though I could tell that wasn't the end of the story.

Don scratched his thighs. "Yeah, all good, but you know how these things go. The way you do when you young. It's in me, you know. This robbing. I think about it and think about it. It like thinking about titties and ass. Every time, after that, when I in a neighborhood working, I can't help but watch. And when I find them drug dealers, I study them until I know them good. Then I put on the Mr. Brown mask and take they money, and take they guns."

"So this is like a second job for you?" I asked. "You know, moonlighting."

Don sucked his teeth. "*Tink* about it," he said, and I could see him tapping his temples in the dark. I imagined his familiar frown. "This is my job. No moonlighting shit. Building on houses is how I go around. Damn, Caesar. This is for real. I bought this boat, and I built my moms a house back home. I send money for everyone, enough so some people can stay in Trinidad and not come here to America where they kill people for talking to the police. All these boys out here, when they come up, they going to private school over in Park Slope or Manhattan or some shit. Then they go home. I do right by them. I do right by lot of people. I take guns, too, and drop 'em off the side of the boat. In these waters here, round my house, they more guns than fish."

Don's proud laughter peeled through the room like a roar. He stood up and led me towards the door. It slid open to a firm breeze and wide open water. Moonlight covered everything. "You be careful, partner," Don said, shaking my hand on the deck. "Real gangsters play rough, you know."

I knew.

**

Don's adolescent security outfit escorted me through the heart of the projects, past small groups gathered on benches in court-yards under the yellow light of street lamps. On a quiet cor-ner under the expressway, they waited in silence until the bus arrived. When the doors hissed open, the boys turned for home.

As the bus jerked and roared through darkened Brooklyn streets, I thought about the gun in my waistband and the viles of crack in my pocket. There was more work to do. More things I needed to know and figure out. Everything was at stake, and things were in motion that I couldn't stop. And I couldn't run. The danger excited me, and the knowledge that change, in some big and unavoidable way, was going to come soon.

By the time I'd made it back to my little block in Clinton Hill, home had never been such a welcome sight. A lamp light was on in the parlor. The iron-gate clicked and clanged. I took the wooden steps two at a time. The front door pushed open at the touch of my key. I stood silent in the vestibule. Entering from the foyer into the front parlor, I called for Colette. No answer. The stairs and the second floor above were dark and silent. I put on the overhead light in the parlor and noticed, as I walked through the rooms, that certain things had been moved, though nothing was missing. An open book spread over the arm of the reading chair in the bay window. In back, the kitchen smelled of roasted potatoes and rosemary. But there was no food on the counter or in the refrigerator. The money and keys I had left were gone.

The house echoed an empty moan as I ascended the stairs to the second floor. Everything was completely black, until I circled around to the next set of stairs. A faint light flickered on the walls leading to the loft. I followed the dancing light to the open room. Dozens of candles in small glass holders were spread out on the floor and on crates and in the window sills. They had all burned nearly to the nub, the wicks dangling toward the pools of melted wax. In the tiny glow, Colette lie on her side, asleep on a blanket in the middle of the room, a button down of mine as a night shirt. An untouched meal was beside her, congealed and cold on a plate. Sitting Indian style by her side, in the shifting and minimal light, I ate the cold roast chicken with Dijon mustard and heavy cream, roasted potatoes and asparagus, took small sips of the Burgundy wine still left in the bottle. Eventually, the candles faded out, one by one, until the room was dark.

I wondered if I should wake Colette, until a blast of light flashed through the street side window, lighting up the block in a red and blue fury. I looked out as a dark car with a silent siren on the dashboard pulled up to the curb across the street, in front of the house next door to Cyrus' place. The siren whooped for a beat then fell silent. In the flashing light, two large figures, without uniforms, got out of the unmarked car. They walked the yard casually toward the front stoop, climbed the stairs, then tried a key in the front door. When it didn't work, they shouldered the door open. A few minutes later, they came down the steps ferrying a man in his pajamas—a guy in his thirties or forties who I saw most days wearing an MTA uniform—across the yard by the elbow. They ducked the man's head and shoved him in the backseat, got into the car. I recognized the driver as the monster security guard from the Art Institute. Now I knew which house on my block Will had bought, and how he dealt with people he wanted out of the way. The car peeled away.

I waited by the window. After fifteen minutes or so, the unmarked car returned to the block and parked in front of the same house. The man in his pajamas got out and hurried inside. He must have gotten the message. The message wasn't lost on me, either. It gave birth to an idea, the kind of idea that took a ton of guts to pull off. But if it worked, I would be free.

I lay down on my bed, considering every angle and option, every potential consequence, until I fell asleep.

**

I dreamed of my brother Angie. He stood on the peak of a giant pine tree and dropped twigs down on me. I began to climb up to him. The sap from the branches clung to my palms, and the pine needles poked at my skin. My thighs burned, but I kept climbing, higher and higher, towards the crystalline sky that haloed my shining brother, who waved me along. When I looked up, shreds of sunlight splintered my eyes. I paddled on, choking on the sticky pine that coated my throat. As I got closer to him, the branches began to fall away, but I persisted until I reached the top. When I got there, my beloved brother turned into a black winged bird and flew away, leaving me atop a tall tree, gasping for breath, all alone with no way down.

*Thursday*

I woke up in the early morning and lifted Colette into bed. She snored gently as I lay by her side, listening to the music playing out back. A trio—sax, bass and drums—practiced in the yard across from mine most mornings. Layers of sound filtered in from outside, mingling together, but somehow separate. I thought of the melody of morning prayers that rose from the nearby mosque. And then I thought of cooking, of building layers of flavor that the tongue picks out, layers that work better together than alone.

My mind traveled back to Carmen, and her family's roadhouse in Louisiana. Each night was like a revival there as the Bayou folks whooped it up at long wooden tables, their animated conservations humming through from the kitchen where I worked.

After the sun plunged into the lake, leaving a hot pink sky behind, the breeze would pick up and a band would take the stage. With the first accordion notes, people would swarm to the worn floor, where they'd dance until closing—cowboy hats and rhinestone buttons, swinging skirts and earrings, hair lifted off the neck, twirling and bouncing of tireless bodies. Every few minutes someone would shout "*De trois!*"

I'd hurry through clean-up to meet Carmen out by the bar. I'd never danced before, but she had taught me to Waltz and Cajun Jitterbug. We moved our feet and hips together, like bass and drums, and sometimes we'd solo on top of that with twists and turns, spins and jumps. Through the trance and rhythm, I'd sometimes see her lips move, and it seemed like she was mouthing a prayer.

Lying in my bed in Brooklyn, listening to the music out back float through my window, I thought about food and music and people, and how well they all went together. An idea came to me, of opening my own place someday, a place where people could eat and dance and be with one another. But before I could do anything so romantic, my plan would have to work out right. I got up, and made for the door.

**

It was another glistening morning. I sat on my stoop and sipped coffee, watching the MTA man move out of the house up the street. He hadn't bothered to pack, just piled his belongings into the back of a rental van. Next door to him, Pimples and High Fade went through their weightlifting routine, glancing over on occasion to stare me down.

A pretty young girl passed by my house. "Hi, mister," she said. She used to greet me like this every day, but I hadn't seen her in a while. She still had her sweet sway, but her gait had slowed and she'd grown quite a bit around the middle. She crossed the street and went up to the fence in her too tight clothes, chatting with High Fade, who looked back at her with disdain. He walked off towards the house, then jerked around on the porch.

"Un-uh!" he yelled. "That ain't on me. That ain't on me."

"I haven't been with nobody else," I heard her plead in an urgent but concealed voice. She rubbed her hands on her thighs and buckled at the knee.

Pimples seemed trapped between laughter and concern as he watched High Fade stomp across the yard to the fence and wave his finger like a gun in the girl's face.

Un-uh," he insisted, looking down at the girl. "Ain't no way. Ain't no way. I put that shits in yo ass!"

The girl shuddered and dropped her head. Teardrops landed

on the sidewalk. She walked away as Pimples began to cackle and hold his belly. "Oh, shit!" he cried. "Oh, shit!"

"I put that shits in yo ass!" High Fade yelled after her. "Bitch!"

Pimples exploded with laughter, then high-fived High Fade, who had resumed lifting. He noticed me looking at him from across the street.

"The fuck you looking at?" he yelled, his voice deepened for effect. "White bitch!"

Pimples stopped laughing and walked up to the fence. They both glared in my direction. The block was silent.

I held up my coffee cup. "Congratulations," I yelled. "You'll make a terrific father."

High Fade started for the gate, but just then the rusty Continental pulled up and cut him off on the sidewalk. Cyrus climbed out and yelled from over the hood. "Get back in that Goddamn yard!" He stomped through the gate and ushered the boys into the house. The door slammed. Raised voices came from inside. The MTA man, watching from the driver's seat of his rental van, shook his head as he started the engine and drove away from the block.

A small smile appeared in my coffee cup. I went inside and woke up Colette. I asked her to go back to her brother's apartment and count up all the paintings that were there, then take one—with a note I would write—to Professor Hamersley at the Art Institute.

While she got herself together, I changed into sweatpants and sneakers and went downstairs. For my plan to succeed, I needed to learn some things about the Montclair Corporation.

\*\*

With my running gear on, I waited in the foyer until Cyrus came out of his house. He lumbered across the yard in an agitated manner and climbed into his car. The rusty Continental chirped its tires and roared down the block. I hit the sidewalk and followed on foot.

The car paused at the corner before turning left. I stayed half a block behind, jogging in place when a red light momentarily halted the Continental's progress. I then had to sprint full speed when we hit a several block stretch of green lights. Overall, though, it wasn't too difficult for me to keep pace with the stop-and-go travel of an automobile on the Brooklyn streets. For the most part, I had to keep myself from getting too close, especially when the rusty Continental would pull up in front of a building and Cyrus would get out. To keep from being recognized, I took turns putting my hood up and down, and taking off my sweatshirt.

For the next two hours, from across corners, or behind cars and trees, I watched Cyrus enter a number of small businesses and residential buildings. The entire time, he carried a large yellow envelope. He was usually inside for about fifteen minutes. Occasionally, I would hear yelling before he came outside and climbed back into the car. He made a dozen or so stops overall, all within the neighborhood, mostly around its downtrodden parameter.

Growing fatigued after a few hours of stealth pursuit, I wasn't prepared when the car suddenly zoomed out of the neighborhood and into the mouth of downtown Brooklyn. I had to bolt for several blocks, dodging pedestrians on the sidewalk and traffic at the corners, just to keep the car in sight.

As the car finally slowed a bit in the maze of downtown traffic, I was able to slow my pace, walking the crowded streets, sweat dripping from my face. I took off my sweatshirt and let my hair down. The sun slowly dried my skin and bright red t-shirt as I covered the triangular circumference of downtown's labyrinth of short and narrow blocks sandwiched between the courts and the open-air mall and the MetroTech center. The buildings were low and mostly brick-faced, though a few taller ones had ornate fronts grayed by grime. There were the predictable low-rent chains, but also authentic shops selling specialties from the Caribbean and Middle East. I passed an Irish pub and an old time New York restaurant where they probably still served hard cocktails and broiled chops for lunch.

I came to a stop as the rusty Continental parked in front of a Roti shop about a block away. Slowly walking closer, I saw that the yellow envelope was still on the dashboard, but that Cyrus was gone.

I looked around. The block's enterprise was monopolized by a small college, its blue awnings fronting several buildings up and down both sides of the street. Students crisscrossed the sleepy one-way; some chatted in small circles. As I stood in the sunlight, a funky girl with a sweet countenance approached on the sidewalk, a Betty Boop bag loaded with textbooks hanging from her shoulder. She wore red Converse high-tops, black leather pants and a white t-shirt with the image of a rapper on the front. A checkered Arabic-styled scarf was knotted on top of her bouncy breasts. She was pretty, and I had no choice but to bother her when I heard the sound of a key chain as Cyrus appeared from behind to pump quarters into a meter.

"And how are you?" I said to the girl.

She stopped and smiled with cautious curiosity, squinting into the sun. "Fine," she said slowly, looking around. She had a thin but smoky voice and was about a head shorter than me and plump in all the right places: ass and tits and cheeks. She swept dark bangs off dark eyebrows with a jeweled hand. A gold boom box ring covered all four of her fingers.

"I like that ring," I said, as Cyrus walked away down the

block. Pub noise came from around the corner as a door opened and closed.

The girl questioned me with a crooked chin.

"Really," I said. "I have the same one, almost wore it today, too."

A dimple pierced her pillow cheeks and a laugh escaped from her sternum. Her skin, the hazy shade of a harvest moon, flushed with a passing of color.

I looked at her bag. "What are you studying?" I asked.

"Criminal Justice," she answered matter-of-fact.

"Gonna be a lawyer?"

"Not sure," she said, tilting her head to one side.

"Come on," I said. "I could probably use you someday."

"Really," she said skeptically. "You don't seem like the type to need a lawyer."

I looked around the block, then back to the girl. "Let me ask you something," I said. She shifted into the shade my body cast and looked up into my eyes. "Where you from?"

"Flatbush," she answered innocently, adjusting her weight to the other hip.

A group of students passed and someone said "Hey, girl," but she didn't respond.

"No," I said. "I mean your family. Where are they from?"

"Well," she said slowly. "My mother is half-Puerto Rican and half-white, and my father's from *Haiti*," she said, a hint of an accent on Haiti. She smiled, pleased with her lineage.

"Quite a combination," I said.

"Thank you," she answered, a little bashful beneath her bangs. "Where you from?" she asked with curious eyes.

"Nowhere," I said. And then her eyes set on something behind me, and the sound of a key chain rattled nearby. Cyrus must have returned, and she was looking at him looking at me. I leaned down and kissed her on the mouth. She tasted like cloves, and didn't kiss me back. But she didn't bite me either, or even pull away. I heard the car door open and slam closed. The keys jangled away. I turned and saw Cyrus, yellow envelope in hand, turn the corner in a hurry.

"You *are* going to need a lawyer someday," the girl said, hands on her hips.

"I told you," I said.

She buttoned her lips into a rosebud as betrayal slanted her eyes.

"Let me explain," I said.

"Nah, nah," she said, a hand still on her hip and the other gyrating towards the distance. "I can see you got something going on here." She looked at the corner that Cyrus had turned.

"Sorry about that," I said turning to leave. "Really."

Her face grew calm. "Be careful," she said.

I promised her I would and hurried on my way, the taste of clove still sweet on my tongue.

**

I caught Cyrus' head reflecting sun on the far corner. I cut across the street. I knew that he had seen me kissing the girl by his car, but that he hadn't yet figured out who I was. However, I knew the sight of me for a second time would change that, so, with my sweatshirt back on, I tied back my hair and folded into the crowd.

Cyrus didn't act as if he was being followed. Instead, he walked along at a brusque clip, turning to comment at every attractive woman he passed. Eventually, at an angular corner, he walked into a building fronted with a large flashing sign offering medical services. The lobby was empty except for a light brown man with a full head of gray hair leaning into a wooden podium and looking down. I walked past unnoticed and ducked into a taco shop.

A few minutes later, with a sack of tacos and a stack of menus, I walked through a glass door into the building's narrow lobby. It was dark and cool. The walls were made of speckled marble.

"Hey there, Papi," I said to the man. He was reading the sports page of the *Post*.

He looked at me with a handsome face with wrinkles around brown eyes.

"*Hola*," he said softly. He wore a light blue uniform shirt with a badge stitched to the breast.

"How's it going?" I asked.

"You know," he said with a shrug. "Trying to make it."

"Me, too," I said, holding up the bag. "Delivery."

"What floor?"

"Fourth," I said.

"Okay, go," he said, returning to his newspaper.

"Can I drop some of these, too?" I asked, showing him the stack of menus. I didn't want him to get curious if I was upstairs for too long.

"OK."

According to the lights above the elevator door, the car was parked on the third floor. I pushed the button and rode alone in the small space up three flights. The doors opened to a quiet hallway over-lit by fluorescent bulbs. A directory on the wall provided no revealing information on the dozen or so offices on the floor. I put my hood up and crept along with the delivery sack held in front of me. From behind closed doors, phones rang and cabinets closed and conversations took place. A familiar voice reached me around the corner.

I went down to the last door. It was the only one without a

name posted, just the number: 312. As I listened to Cyrus converse with another man, there was something about the second voice that was familiar, something about the tone that I couldn't quite place. The voices rose and fell as if they were arguing or jostling one another. I could tell by the abruptness of the volley that the conversation was ending. Footsteps approached the door. My pores opened up as my heart began to race. The hallway was long, but there was a bathroom one door down on the other side. I rushed over and turned the knob, but it was locked. I put my shoulder into the door, but the jamb only rattled. I hurried down the corridor and pounded on number 311. No answer, though I could hear someone inside warbling in a loud and horrible accent. I knocked again as the door down the hall opened and I heard Cyrus bid his farewell as he exited. Just then, the door to number 311 opened to a red faced man in a blue striped suit.

"You're not the cleaning lady!" the man raged in my face. He was disheveled and blinking. Booze colored his breath as I stepped past him into the cluttered foyer of a dingy office space. There was another room in back and no one else around. "Where's the cleaning lady?" he demanded.

"She'll be here in a minute," I said, extending the sack. "Eat these."

"What is this?" he spat through floundering lips. "I call for cleaning lady!"

I shoved the sack into his hand, walked out the door, then quietly slipped back down the hall. There was no name on the directory next to the office number where Cyrus had been. I took the stairs and sidled up to the man at the podium. I offered him a crisp twenty in exchange for the name of the company in 312.

His eyes went wide and he held up his hands. "No, no, Papi," he said. "I don't know nothing about that." His face grew stern. "I thought you were here for delivery?" He stepped from behind the podium with a baseball bat in his hand. He followed me out the door and onto the sidewalk where I disappeared into the pedestrian traffic and headed towards home.

**

On the walk back to Clinton Hill, I tried to place the mysterious voice. Cyrus worked for someone familiar, and they were holed up in an out of the way and anonymous office with a quiet security force guarding them.

By the time I made it back to my block, the sun had passed overhead. I sat on my steps in the midday shade. Kids on the other side of the street played a game of chase up and down the block. They squealed and screamed as they tagged and dodged each other. In the cool of my porch, I leaned my head against the railing and closed my eyes. The memory of childhood surrounded me.

**

Sallie was wearing a dirty t-shirt and jeans torn at the knees, his face smeared with blood, his eyes alive with suffering. We were out back of our house, by the boxing ring made of steel drum corners looped with rope that my father had built. The grass within the ring had been worn into hard dirt. My father, in work boots and boxing gloves, was trying to coax Sallie back into the ring with insults. He called his son Nancy boy and asked if he had hurt his vagina, said he'd never amount to nothing if he didn't learn to take a punch. But Sallie didn't budge. He stood in the yard and wiped blood from his nose with the back of his glove. A streak of crimson covered one eye and thickened his hair. "Fuck it, then," our father finally said, "I'm thirsty anyway."

He stripped off the gloves, hopped on his motorcycle and headed for town. When the sound of the engine cleared the block,
Sallie set his eyes on me. He was twelve and I was just seven,
and while he didn't come for me that day, I knew it was only a
matter of time.

That summer, Sallie cleaned out a forgotten shed in the far
corner of the yard. He got a bench press and a weight bar, pried
manhole covers straight from the street and drilled them through
to make plates, and hung straps from the ceiling for pull-ups. He
practically lived in that shed. Day and night, clanging and bang-
ing and grunting noises came from inside that rusty hole, until
Sallie would emerge shirtless and sweaty, veins bulging all over
his ballooning upper body.

Not lean like the other Stiles men, Sallie took from my
mother's stock and adopted the form of a bull. Seeing him in
the homemade ring with my father was like watching an animal
against a matador. Sallie would charge and swing and usually
miss with great might, and then my father would pick him apart
with long jabs, precise and relentless, going after the same spot
on Sallie's chin or cheek or nose over and over again, trying to
teach the boy a lesson. It was painful to watch: Sallie full of fury,
unable to even pin our lanky father in a corner. The man moved
like a magician, even in work boots, and fighting him was like
battling a ghost. You could practically see Sallie's sanity slipping
through the ropes. And eventually his madness came for me.

Any time I was near him, as long as our parents weren't
around, he'd bash me. And, since our father wasn't around much,
and our mother worked long and odd hours at a diner, I was
alone a lot of time. I would be eating cereal in the morning, by
myself at the kitchen table, and end up on the floor with a bleeding ear. I hid when I could from him, but, living in the same
house, going to the same school, he would inevitably find me.

As a result of Sallie's steady beatings, I had a constant headache throughout junior high, as well as some cracked ribs, a busted ear drum, a twice-broken nose and a cracked canine.

The only thing that saved my life was Angie. Without a mother or father to protect me, only my brother's charms, his preternatural ease, kept me alive. He could disarm Sallie with a bit of deprecation and dash. "Come on, big man," he'd say. "Leave the shit stain alone." And Sallie would—until that train came and Angie wasn't around to protect me anymore.

While Sallie had always been cut from some bizarre, deranged cloth, he got even worse after Angie died. Though I'd never seen him care about anything or anyone before, he became obsessed with knowing what had really happened to his brother. He needed revenge like he needed to breathe. He asked everyone from the neighborhood, from the town, what had happened that afternoon by the tracks. He had a twisted sense of justice, and someone had to pay for Angie's death. Even Steven, as he would say. But no one knew the truth but me, and I hid my secrets from Sallie like I hid myself from him. I knew it was just a matter of time until he found out—until something got in the way.

I remember the scream from my mother when she found him on the living room floor, face down and soaked in blood from his jacket to his jeans. She stood there, still and white as a statue, her mouth open with a hand held out to her son, as if she were the one who had stabbed him all those times in the back.

There had been a fight outside a bar. Sallie had mauled some poor bastard, pounding him with punches from his sledgehammer fists, bashing his head on the ground. Just before the sirens came, one of the guy's friends leapt out of the crowd and wailed Sallie on the back with a closed hand, a hand that held a three-inch blade. Thick leather is what saved Sallie's life. He managed to escape the scene and made it home before falling unconscious on the living room floor, where my mother found him when she returned from an evening shift at the diner.

Hearing her scream, I ran downstairs and saw Sallie on the blood-stained carpet. I hoped he was dead, but then I saw blood pump slowly through the holes in his body. My mother told me to call an ambulance. I did, then went back to my room and stayed there until the house was empty. My mother came home the next morning from the hospital and told me that Sallie would live. The doctors called it a miracle, but no one else did. Not even my mother, who visited him less and less as he recovered.

When Sallie got out of the hospital two months later, I was gone. With my knife in one pocket and my money in the other, I hopped that train and headed away from home. My mother begged me in her letters to come back. She said Sallie had changed, that he was quiet now and focused on his job fixing cars at a garage in town. I wanted to believe her, but I knew that mothers, even a sharp one like my own, could be blind to the sins of their sons.

I was right about that, as Sallie methodically chased the guy with the three-inch blade all over Jersey. After two years, he found him down by the shore, outside a check cashing place. It took three cops to pull Sallie off of him, but the damage was already done. The man was left an imbecile, and minus one eye. They sentenced Sallie to fifteen years, and I figured he'd see every minute of it. But I was wrong about that.

**

I decided to walk around the neighborhood to try and clear my head. I knew I couldn't hide from Sallie—he was relentless, as stubborn as he was stupid, and as stupid as he was cruel. He wouldn't go away, at least not on his own. And there was no Angie to protect me anymore.

Under a naked blue sky, I walked through the brownstone streets, until I reached a playground. In a shaded area, I cranked pull-ups on the monkey bars and did push-ups off the black-top. The toothless temperature made no impression on my skin. Through the chatter of childhood activity, I thought about my clever yet extremely dangerous plan. Fucking with Sallie was not the smart thing to do, and if my plan didn't work, I knew he really would kill me this time. My heart beat fast. My mind raced. I gripped the park fence, starring at the sidewalk through metal bars, wrestling with the reality of my brother being out of jail, until the dreary girl from the Art Institute trudged past.

She moved without lateral motion or haste, her path slow and straight as the progress of a freight train. I left the playground and followed her for a few blocks, until she arrived at Washington Avenue. Beside a multi-unit apartment building loomed the Jefferson Hotel, a battered brownstone-turned-rooming house with a torn green awning extending from the front door to the curb. In the parlor floor window, a neon sign declared "Vacancy" while a plastic sign advertised daily and hourly rates.

The girl walked under the green awning and through the glass door. After waiting a few minutes, I followed her in. At the end of a narrow foyer, lit by a small lamp, a man behind a wooden counter leafed through a snatch magazine. I coughed. He squinted from a bulldog's face.

"Which room did she go to?" I asked. With my eyes, I followed the steps up a stairwell that curled out of sight.

"Huh?" the man asked, slowly scratching his crinkled hair.

"My girlfriend," I said. "She just came in. I was parking the car." I held my hand out to the side to indicate her height. "White girl, black clothes."

The counter man studied me. "She didn't say nothing about you."

"That would be her," I said.

He nodded, then broke into a smile. "I know the type," he said. "She up in 204."

I thanked him and bound up the stairs.

The door to 204 was open, and four figures were spread around the disheveled, dark room. The girl and the Asian guys from the Mexican restaurant sat silently along the side of the bed. They didn't notice when I entered, but someone else did. "Who the fuck is you?" a man growled. He sat in the corner of the room, grizzly and bedraggled, reeking of body odor and urine and the burnt smell that came from the glass pipe in his hand.

I quickly crossed the room and pulled up the shades. In the flood of light, as the crack head and the college students covered their eyes like vampires, Jean-Baptist Rennet came in from the bathroom. He saw me, and immediately bolted out the door. The girl let loose a wild, happy howl that chased me down the stairs.

I followed the artist down and out the front door. On the sidewalk, he ran like a mad man, stumbling forward and checking over his shoulder. I called out for him to stop, but he kept going. He turned into the playground and barreled through the children. Snagged by the ropes of a double-dutch session, the girls screamed at him as he tore away towards the hoop game. I followed through the screams and jokes, the pandemonium of playground noise, across the basketball court and out of the park. He daringly crossed the road in front of traffic to create some distance between us.

Around the next corner, I caught a glimpse of his head descending the subway stairs. I paddled down the steps, hopped the turnstile and ran toward the Coney Island bound side. The platform was empty. The shaded air chilled the sweat on my back and neck as I peered around each column and down the darkened tunnels on either end of the platform. The wall tiles gleamed back, revealing no shadows.

A man in a reflective orange vest wearing headphones came from the opposite end, sweeping and singing an Al Green tune. I watched until his head acknowledged something behind a post. He stepped back. I sprinted down the platform. The lights from the tiles reflected onto Jean-Baptist jumping onto the tracks. The rumble of a train came from deep down the tunnel. He stepped over the rails and ducked under beams as he crossed ahead of the oncoming train. I leaped down and fell to one knee. The light from the rushing train blinded me. The horn blew. I stood straight. The wind pushed back my hair, filling my nose with sour dust. I thought of my brother and his death on the tracks. Something told me to move. I slipped to the side just in time to see the metal cars flashing past.

Once the train had left the station, I crossed over the collection of rails and pushed myself back onto the platform. On the landing, a couple shook their heads. I raced beside the tiles towards the steps of the subway station, feeling filthy and dazed, my lungs jabbed with pain. I took the steps two at a time. Outside, the sun was bright and warm. I looked around. On the next corner, a hat flew in the air. "My Lord!" a woman screamed.

I made for the corner and leapt over someone on the ground. "Young man!" the figure cried as Jean-Baptist ran straight through the light without slowing. "Young man!" the voice came again from behind. It was a familiar voice. I watched Jean-Baptist disappear around a corner. I turned and walked back to the woman on the ground.

"You all right, Reverend?" I asked. My lungs felt torn and I wheezed between words.

"Young man," she repeated, furious and confused. I held out my hand, but she helped herself up. "What on God's earth are you up to?" She brushed off the backside of her brown tweed suit and stood tall with the church at her back. It was an enormous sandstone structure that cleaved the corner like a ship run ashore. I picked up her hat, a straw number with a synthetic sunflower above the curled brim.

"You all right?" I asked, gathering my breath.

"I'm fine," she said curtly. "I've faced down all sorts of hatred, and I'm still here today. I don't need help picking myself up. No sir. Maybe it's you who needs help—a grown man out here, chasing someone down the sidewalk in the middle of the day, with no regard for citizens! I ask again, what on God's earth are you doing?"

"I'm sorry, Reverend," I said. "It's a long story."

"Maybe you should tell it then," she said, her voice smoothing out. "Hear how this story of yours sounds out loud."

I thought about that, about telling her my story, the story of my family, my mother's mother and the curse she brought from Italy, about my mother and father, my brother Angie and my brother Sallie and my wandering around America, how I got to Brooklyn and why I was helping the French girl and everything else that had led me to this corner, right there and then, in front of this glorious church, being coaxed towards a confession by a woman of God.

Instead, I handed the reverend her back her hat and walked away.

**

Howlin' Wolf growled regret over a wicked guitar riff as I entered The Notch, sweaty and late. The joint was a mess. The Captain looked worse.

"The hell you been, Stiles?" he barked. He was behind the bar, his cap pushed back on his head, the fluster all over his face reminding me of the day we first met.

"Sorry," I said. "Something came up, an emergency."

"Emergency my ass," the Captain said. "You ain't been a minute late since the day I took you on, and now two days in a row, you come in way past time and then not at all. "Naw, naw," he said, shaking his head, leaning his hands into the bar. "Something going on Stiles, and I don't care what it is, but it need to stop. I make myself heard?"

"The delivery come?" I asked him.

The Captain motioned towards a pile of sealed boxes by the stairs. I asked if he checked the veal—I had had to send the last delivery back due to spoil.

"Me?" he asked. "Did *I* check the God damn veal?" He gestured wildly, patting himself down and throwing his hands in the air. He pointed at me across the bar. "*That's* your job Stiles, not mine. You get paid to be here to make sure them motherfuckers bring the right veal and whatever else you order. *That's* your job, Stiles, not mine. You hear?"

I heard, as did someone else.

"I catch you at a bad time, Claire?" the voice asked, deep and condescending. Cyrus had his wide hands out to the side, the light shining off his shaved head, a shit eating grin under his horseshoe mustache. I didn't know that he knew the Captain—or that the Captain's name was Claire.

The Captain licked his thick lips. "What you want?"

"I need to see you, man," Cyrus said. "Alone. It's important."

Shaking his head, the Captain waved him toward the back. The loaded key ring on Cyrus' belt jangled as he rolled through the restaurant like he'd been in a thousand times, though I'd never seen him here before. The big stone in his ear winked as he passed. He didn't look at me at all. The Captain joined him in the back.

I carried the boxes up the stairs and unloaded the contents. As I pounded veal to the rhythm of "Killing Floor," I remembered when I discovered the blues.

**

In Austin, I built houses and haunted bars. The town felt like an oasis within the oppression that is Texas. The girls from the university were wild and friendly, and there was music everywhere.

It was there that I met a musician named Macie Turner. He wore an alligator vest, and his braided hair hung like a gray mane down his back. A feather dangled from his right ear. A big, left-handed man, one part Indian and three parts black, he told me he came from the two most persecuted peoples in history, after the Jews. I asked him about the Irish, and he said they were fourth.

Macie knew hundreds of songs, all blues, none of them his own. He said that that didn't matter because nothing was original, only taken from other stuff. He said that songs were stories, which made him a storyteller, and that stories were clues to understanding life. He told his tales on a circuit round the American south from Texas and Arkansas through Mississippi and Louisiana. He traveled alone and he traveled by train. Said he'd been at it for one hundred years.

He played an antique Martin guitar slung across his waist, his big boot tapping out time while his deep voice—which needed no amplification—belted out the tunes. He was known by everyone in Austin, so when word spread that Macy was in town, he'd draw a big crowd wherever he played.

Being two loners in a fraternal town, we became fast friends. Some nights, after the bars closed and the music went silent, the two of us would go back to the empty houses where I worked days and slept on lonely nights. We would sit in the frame of houses without walls, or roofs, and he'd tell me stories under the Texas sky rung with stars. He told me the Devil lived on a hilltop in Mississippi and that New Orleans was a city kept afloat by the souls of slave owners. He said Muddy Waters was in heaven and Howlin' Wolf was in hell, and that they'd wrestle on nights when there was a three-quarter moon. He said his father was a sharecropper who married a half-Seminole from Tallahassee, and that his mother had sown herself into a cotton kite and flown away when he was four years old. He told me he was the youngest of eleven and left home at age eight because he'd come to believe that the Devil preyed on unloved children. He ended up in a Biloxi whorehouse where the prostitutes raised him and the johns taught him their songs. At the age of thirteen, after being raised right by the love of countless women and many rambling men, he left the whorehouse to wander the country, telling stories and saving souls. I told Macie my story, and he cried in the blue light of a west Texas dawn. He said I might still be saved.

We set off to traveling together. He played his guitar and I listened from the dusty corners of warbling trains and juke joints buried deep in the woods. He sang of floods and drought, of curses and cures, of little girls and grown women, of cheating men and decent men. There were songs about regret and songs about redemption, about pleasure and pain, walking and rolling and moving on. Love in vein and love gone wrong. His songs taught me that men were restless souls chased by the past after something that couldn't be found. He said the key to salvation was in our hearts and not in our feet. And that something could be learned by singing the blues. God's mercy, he told me, found every man in a moment of grace, and the earlier you found that grace, the better man you'd become.

After a turn through the circuit, on our way back to Texas,

we stopped at a roadhouse in Louisiana where I met the owner's daughter, a Bayou child named Carmen with corkscrew hair and green apple eyes. She asked me to dance a Cajun jitterbug. Macie left me there that night, without saying goodbye. He must have thought I'd be saved by her grace. But he was wrong.

**

By the time the Captain walked Cyrus to the front door and out to the curb, the wait staff had arrived and the tables were set. Jacqui poured Prosecco for a pretty woman at the bar. The staff spoke quietly among themselves, staying busy with small tasks while waiting for the crowd to arrive.

In the kitchen, pots of water boiled and olive oil shimmered. Twenty-five veal cutlets had been tenderized and coated in bread crumbs, Parmesan, and oregano. I pan fried a large one and lay a trail of tomato and greens down the middle. As I ate, I wondered if it would be my last meal at The Notch. The Captain had a short rope, which he hung people with all the time.

I wouldn't have much time to consider getting fired as this was a Thursday, and Thursdays hopped at The Notch. This Thursday, a few days before a holiday, turned out to be especially busy. Everything moved all night long. Constant motion and sound. The special was 86'd by nine-thirty. People lingered and drank until midnight.

After cleaning up the kitchen, I was heading for home when the Captain called me to his table in the front window. Jacqui brought over a Bass Ale and a snifter of cognac. There was no music playing.

"What's going on with you, son?" the Captain asked.

I sipped my beer and said nothing.

"Come on, Stiles," the Captain said, leaning back into his wooden seat. "Something different with you. I can tell. Ever since that French filly come in here, something been going on, and I want to know what it is."

I wanted to know why he wanted to know.

"Because," he said. "I'm concerned."

My look must have said I didn't believe him.

"Come on now, Stiles," he said, waving his hand. "You don't need to worry about all that before. That's just how people talk sometimes when they get hot. It don't mean nothing. I've never been one to show too much emotion, too much care—it gets you burned in this business. I know that after all these years. You know that, too, don't 'cha Stiles? Yeah, I could tell that from the first time you come in here, that you been around, seen some things. That's why I took you on. I said to myself, now here's a young man who knows how it works. And you know what? I was right. You do know how it works. You come in on time, do your job, do it damn well, don't take no mess from no one, and you make things happen. You been an asset to me, a big one, and I've enjoyed having you around, but when I see something change all the sudden I need to ask what's going on. I need to know what's happening with my man." He raised his eyebrows and took a sip of cognac. I smelled liquor fumes and the underbelly of oak.

"You want to know what's going on with me?" I asked.

"Yeah," he said, sitting up, putting his elbows on the table. "Maybe I can help."

"And how's that?"

"I don't know," he said, shrugging with feigned modesty. "I been around a while, know some people 'round here. If you in some trouble, I could probably get you out."

"I'm not in any trouble."

"No?" he asked, tilting his head. "Then it got to have something to do with that French girl. She got you running around or whatever, messing up your work." He raised his brow and leaned forward, looking at me almost like a father. "Pussy do that to you, son. Pussy is magic. Especially that sweet *éclair* I imagine little Frenchy got."

I had to laugh at that one.

"Yes, sir," he said, laughing, too. "Ain't nothing like a fine piece a pussy to make a grown man lose his mind!" He smacked the table and we laughed some more. It felt good to laugh with the Captain, though I knew it wasn't authentic.

"Don't worry about Saturday," I said. "I know it's a big night. I'll be here, and on time."

"*Sheet,*" he said. "I'm not worried about all that. I'm not worried about that at all. It's you I'm worried about. This is a funny neighborhood, Stiles. Got its own rules, and it's best, if you ain't in the mix, to stay clear of things. Stay out the way. Know what I'm saying?"

Now I did. And now I knew why Cyrus had come by the bar. And the mysterious voice he had spoken to behind the closed door in downtown Brooklyn finally came to me: it was Montgomery—the Captain's accountant. They were partners. Montgomery and Claire. The Montclair Corporation. All those properties belonged to them. Cyrus worked for the Captain and Montgomery, and he had come to the bar to complain about me. I was becoming a nuisance. Maybe just with the kids, or maybe Cyrus had spotted me following him. Or the security guard at the office in downtown had reported my inquiry, and they now knew I'd been poking around. I couldn't know for sure. But what I did know for sure was that I had just been given a warning. A gentle warning, though I imagined the next time wouldn't be so nice.

I shook my empty beer bottle and put it on the table. "Thanks for the advice," I said.

"Anytime, son," the Captain said. "Anytime."

**

I walked home in the soft breath of the late evening. The breeze skirted my skin like cloth. The sky was hazy with stars. My block was quiet and I hoped to find Colette waiting on the stoop, her hands between her knees, smiling, slow dragging on a cigarette and longing for me.

However, the stoop was empty and the house seemed dark until I stood right in front and noticed a hint of light coming from the kitchen in the back. I thought of another late night meal with Colette. Hoping to surprise her in the kitchen, I disappeared into the alley, slipping past Angel's dark windows. From the back garden, I saw dim light from my kitchen shining through the back window onto the terrace, leaving a silhouette on the surface. I quietly climbed the back stairs, panting and anxious, and looked through the kitchen window. The orange man sat on a stool, smoking a cigarette. My heart sank, followed by a rush of rage. I thought about killing him, of waiting in the shadows with my knife, then splitting him like an Easter lamb. Before I could do anything, though, the door opened and the orange man flicked his cigarette into the garden and waved me inside.

"Thanks for having me," I said, entering my kitchen. The dimmer on the overhead lights had been lowered to minimum visibility. It would have been romantic, if it wasn't for the company.

The orange man nodded and gestured towards the single stool. The lighting arrangement made it hard to see his face.

"Something to drink?" I asked.

He stared for a moment as his mouth hooked down. "Margarita," he said. "Easy on the salt." A flash of white teeth appeared in the dark.

I took two glasses and a bottle of Kentucky mash from the cupboard. I slid the stool across the tiled floor towards my guest, filled a glass and passed it over the island. He took the glass and sniffed the liquor. On the other side of the island, in front of the knife drawer, I poured myself a drink. The orange man sat on the stool and sighed. His figure cast a ghostly shadow on the walls.

"I find you interesting," he said.

"And how's that?" I asked. The whiskey tasted sour and strong, mellow in the belly.

The orange man took a sip of his drink and put the glass down. He pulled out a cigarette and dropped the match into the glass, jetting smoke through his nose. Not a whiskey man, I gathered.

"There's something about you I admire," he said, "and something I pity."

I, on the other hand, enjoyed whiskey. I sipped some more, letting the burn rise in my chest and vent out my nose. It tasted of cherry oak and sugar and made my mouth dry.

"This whole situation with Martina has me curious," he said, tapping his fingertips together. "She had many, many admirers, but you are the only one I can't say for certain, yes or no, because there seems to be no reason. No logic. Why send someone away, but not be with her? You are defeating your own purpose. A stupid person might do that, but you are not stupid. When I look at someone, I ask: What do they want? And often it comes to sex and money. And safety, too, of course. I am being reductive, but that, ultimately, in some form or another, is what people like you live for. And this, I've seen many, many times, is what people like you die for, also. But in your case, if you were to send Martina away, you would be denying yourself sex and money, and, of course, making yourself incredibly unsafe. So here is my confusion, because I think you did it, but I can't figure out why, and I can't kill a man without being certain, and I can't be certain without knowing why."

I refilled my glass as the orange man continued. "A man is nothing more than his past. And this is where I get confused because I can't completely find your past. Since the age of fifteen, until recently, you had been a ghost. No school records. No bank account. No permanent address. No taxes. You reappear two years ago to bury your mother. You inherit a house and some money. You open a bank account and buy another house. This house. The activity in your account is not unusual. There is a job at the restaurant from which you deposit cash, roughly the same amount every two weeks, and a check every month from an Angela Peyton, whom I assume is the girl downstairs. You have much more money coming in than going out. You are successful. But you do stupid things. And what is it from your past that makes you do stupid things? Like helping this pathetic French girl."

The orange man smiled, his teeth white and capped. I fought the choking urge in my throat, tipped open the knife drawer.

"Yes, I met her earlier," he said. "She walked right in like this was her house. She was terribly scared to find me here, but she eventually calmed down and told me her situation."

I leaned forward and slipped a long, sharp carving blade from the drawer, concealing it against my forearm.

"And her brother is the one with the drugs you asked me about?"

I nodded.

"They are both very desperate then."

"Yeah, they are," I said.

"He is quite talented, I understand. But he is not fit for the world he admires. Fascination will be his demise. I see his type often."

"Some conversation you had," I said.

"I speak many languages," the orange man responded without expression. "The girl had a lot to say."

"Where is she?"

The orange man shook his orange head in the dim light of my kitchen. "I sent her away. Nice girl like that doesn't need to be around people like me for too long."

I said nothing.

"She brought you flowers," he said, glancing towards the sunflowers that lay on the floor, where Colette had most likely dropped them upon finding the orange man in my kitchen. The thick green stems were snapped six inches below the yellow face ringed with black petals. She must have picked them from an open lot.

The orange man suddenly stood up, the stool squawking across the tiles.

"Put back the knife," he said.

I did, as fear and shame prickled across my hairline, where a string of sweat beads surfaced.

We exchanged stares. The orange man reached inside his jacket. Adrenalin jolted my body, sending the sweat cascading down my face. He flipped a stuffed envelope on the counter. "And how does any of this with the girl involve the corporation you asked me about?"

"I'm not sure," I sighed, curious and relieved.

He angled his nose towards the envelope. "Be careful," he said. "You have sex and money, but your safety is not as certain."

I told him I understood.

He paused for a long time to read my eyes. "I don't want to see you again," he abruptly said, then walked out the back door, down the wrought-iron steps, and through the shadows of the alley.

I enjoyed a big breath of freedom and wondered if God's mercy had just been delivered in the form of a surgically reconstructed foreigner who spoke without an accent. I picked up the sunflowers, put them in a spaghetti container with a few inches of water and placed them in the center of the island. The flowers would be gone soon, I knew, but I'd enjoy them while they lasted.

I emptied the envelope the orange man had left and began reading about the Montclair Corporation. It was incredible information, more than enough to complete my plan. I read it over and over until I folded my arms on the counter and dropped into sleep, my face turned toward the brilliant flowers.

**

I dreamed of escape in Montreal. Sun shined and the snow receded as I searched the wet city in search of Martina. In a quiet neighborhood, on a store-lined street, she walked alone, her platinum hair bouncing down the back of a turtleneck sweater. Wearing boots and tights and a wool skirt, she carried designer shopping bags in both hands. I called out. She turned and stared, looking alive and free, innocent as the doves that cooed in the eaves above her head. Her face conveyed an honest mistake and she walked away. But as her boots clicked the sidewalk, her head turned back in my direction and a hint of a smile appeared in her eyes. I crossed the glistening street and followed through the strange sounds and smells of a foreign city. At a corner, she chatted with an elderly woman who pointed in the opposite direction. I followed Martina towards a large dome teeming with people. Inside the train terminal, we walked on marble floors, together, but separated by several feet. People passed right through us. Announcements in French crackled from a speaker. Down the stairs were cavernous tunnels, chilled and rank and completely abandoned. Retired trains sat dormant on the tracks. Martina stopped in the middle of a platform and turned to me. She dropped her bags and smiled as if she had been waiting for me all along. I kissed her mouth, tasted her tongue, and refused to wake up, even though I knew it was all just a dream. Martina was nowhere near Montreal. She was nowhere I could ever guess, or tell anyone. But she was free.

*Friday*

The morning air was bright with springtime. I walked the quiet streets to the heights, the wide sidewalks deserted except for dogs and their walkers, and the occasional jogger. White light reflected off still cars as majestic trees quivered in the breeze. The buildings, a mixture of brownstones and limestones and brick, were set far back from the sidewalk.

On one particularly grand block, three stand-alone mansions stood royally alongside one another: a white Victorian with ornate carvings on its façade; a brown brick Romanesque with a slanted copper roof and pointed eaves; and a brownstone-faced structure with columns in its broad stoop. Each house was fronted by an iron gate, and had a carriage house in back.

I turned two corners and knocked on the red front door of a restored carriage behind the Romanesque. Will answered my knock wearing a shiny sweat suit, a tennis racket in his hand.

"Oh, hey, Stiles," he said after a pause. "Sorry, man. I thought you were somebody else."

"What?" I said, with my hands out. "We didn't have a match this morning?"

Will crinkled his brow, gave me a smile and a huff. "So, what's up, man?"

"Can I talk to you for a minute?"

He read that I was there for business and invited me in. The large front room was dark, with African sculptures on the walls and leather furniture on the wooden floors forming a U around a big TV on a stand in the corner next to a stereo system flashing with green and red lights. Just before the open kitchen, lit in back by a tiled splash, spiraled a staircase onto a darkened landing. We passed through the ground floor to a door in back which opened to a large, bare room with no windows, a cement floor and a huge desk in the middle. Diplomas and certificates rested on top of file cabinets, and tennis balls littered the floor beneath a neatly painted net against the far wall.

Will sat on his desk, while I leaned against the cool wall.

"What can I do for you, Mr. Stiles?" he asked in an officious tone.

"I saw that your tenant moved out," I said.

"Which one?"

"The one that doesn't pay his rent," I said, reminding him of my address.

Will grimaced. "I didn't want to do that, man," he said shaking his head. "I didn't. I offered the man a month free so that he could have some time to find another space, but he wouldn't take it. You know, I can't stand the welfare culture around here. All these handouts people take, act like they deserve it. I can't stand that shit, man. It don't get no one nowhere."

He tried to look mad, but I could sense his shame. I didn't say anything. "It ain't right," he added, shaking his head. Then, after a moment of silence, he started to tell me his story. I knew it already, as he'd told it to me before, several times, at the bar, but I let him regale me again. There's nothing a big ego needs more than a big ear, and I was going to need Will and his ear on my side.

I heard, again, about his middle-class childhood in a neighborhood on the backside of Queens. About how he was raised by Guyanese immigrants, a bus driver and a secretary. How he went to college in Brooklyn and met a girl who taught him to play tennis on the courts of a park in an old rundown, though architecturally gorgeous, African American neighborhood, and how, even then, he could see that the future lie in developing the neighborhood.

After college he went to law school, worked a few years to build up some credit, then took out a loan to buy a foreclosed mansion in the same neighborhood, a mansion stacked with winos and junkies that the city was in no rush to kick out, so he had to do what he had to do. This was when he put his team together, starting with a fraternity brother from college, a former football player who worked for the NYPD and moonlighted as a security guard at an art school in the very neighborhood in which Will had bought his dilapidated mansion. After the winos and junkies were gone, Will had the building cleaned up and divided into a dozen separate and sparkling apartments, selling each unit himself because he didn't need a real estate agent taking twenty percent of his profit. The first sale paid back the loan, the second covered the renovation of the carriage house, and the rest went into Will's growing pocket.

And he kept going from there, buying and fixing and selling. The neighborhood was changing, as he had predicted, and he had been smart enough to be ahead of that change. The art school's endowment had doubled and they were driving much of the development, but it was also people with money from Manhattan looking for some space and beauty outside of the so-called city. Too liberal or too hip for the suburbs, it was only a matter of time before they started pouring into Brooklyn; therefore, it was only a matter of time before big time developers came in and started sucking up blocks, overbuilding and changing the flavor, which was why he had to deal the way he did with those who stood in his way. There were forces against him. He brought up the Montclair Corporation and mentioned how he'd been receiving threats: anonymous phone calls and dark letters. Recently, a monkey wrench had crashed through his front window, which was why his buddy the football player/cop/security guard had been sleeping on his couch for the past month. His friendship with the cop and the part about the threats were things he had never told me before.

Will's combination of greed, fear and impatience fit perfectly into my plan. So I made him an indecent offer that his ego couldn't refuse. He smiled, impressed with my savvy, and shook his head. "Damn, guy," he said. "That's some valuable information right there."

"Million dollar," I joked.

After shaking hands, we negotiated a second, far more legitimate business arrangement.

**

I left Will's place, caught the subway into Manhattan, then a commuter train out to northern New Jersey. Once the train emerged from the caverns of the city and made its way through the sprawl of its ramparts across the river, the landscape changed. Sleepy towns with modest signs now marked the platforms, while in-between those towns the trees came up close to the tracks in stretches of pine and birch. Small hills smoked yellow in the sunlight as hawks soared high overhead. Eventually, the conductor called out my hometown. I got off the train, and headed down the stairs of the station.

The town's main drag stretched across a slight valley, bulbous tree cover lining the distance beyond a strip of five-and-dimes, delis and hair salons. Not much had changed since I was a kid. In the same candy shop I had once shoplifted from, old men still sat on button stools sipping egg creams and talking about the news. The corner garage, where Sallie used to work, had cars stacked for repair. Across the street from the garage was the only place in the town with a liquor license, an inn where the town's two major roads met. The inn had a slanted "for sale" sign in the corner of a front window. Upstairs, behind a facade of stucco and wood, was the office of Andrew R. Alvino, my lawyer.

I had grown up with Andy. We had been in the same class, and once a year I went to his house for a birthday party where we played games and watched movies and ate cake and candy. He never stepped foot in my house, though—the train tracks had kept us separated, in more ways than one. Though his parents, like mine and many others from the town, had come to north Jersey from upper Manhattan or the Bronx, the difference between me and Andy was that his father had been a lawyer, not a drunk carpenter with a failed dream of being a boxer, his mother a school teacher, not a waitress trying to hold two jobs and a family together.

His brick walled office was lined with framed certificates and volumes of legal matter. Pictures of him and his wife and their three kids graced his mahogany desk. It seemed like they'd been to lots of places, from the mountains to the sea. Golf clubs waited in the corner by the water cooler. Andy looked fit in a button down shirt and factory-faded jeans.

We started off with some polite chitchat, about the town, and the kids we used to know, the kids we used to be, before moving on to more serious matters: my house, and how property values were rising in commuter towns like this one. We talked about my dead brother, and the one that was still alive, and the legalities of real estate transactions. When we were done, I thanked Andy for his time and handed him an envelope that he handed back. He told me the real bill would come later, when the deal was done. As an alternative, he said I could pay him back by buying that dump of an inn downstairs and firing the chef. He gave me his business card and walked me to the door. We agreed to talk again soon.

**

The road to my old neighborhood was canopied by maples. I remembered sunlight bathing the streets when I was a kid. Things change. Trees grow. Many of the houses had either new facades, or extensions in back, and, with all the growth cleared away, they seemed farther apart than I recalled as a kid. It was almost like the neighborhood had grown up. Or maybe it was just me.

I cut through someone's backyard and walked along the train tracks. The abandoned boxcars from my childhood were long gone, and I could now look pretty far in either direction as the rails disappeared west towards Pennsylvania on my right, east toward New York City on my left. I went left towards the city, toward the valley around the bend, the valley where Angie had died. Before the bend, I turned down a dirt road with the barb-wired fence of an electrical plant on one side and the backs of houses on the other. Dead pine needles crunched underfoot. I hopped a metal barrier rope onto the dead end. Two story houses, A-framed and aluminum-sided, like models in a board game, stood side-by-side, separated by yards.

I stood on the manhole cover that had served as home plate and remembered my youth spent on that dead end, playing stick ball, having foot races or rock fights, wrestling with the neighborhood kids or just sitting on the curb waiting for my father to come home. I'd sit there for what felt like hours, the summer that he left, rubbing the asphalt with my shoe, waiting for the sound of his motorcycle in the distance. Everything was quiet now as I stood in the middle of the empty street.

The yard of the second house in from the dead end was covered in dead leaves and heavy grass. The boarded up windows and chained front door made it appear haunted, probably inspiring fantasies in the local children and property value concerns for their parents. This was my house.

I borrowed equipment and supplies from an old neighbor and spent the rest of the afternoon cleaning up the yard. After I was done, I went inside, and opened up all the windows to clear out the dead air. The interior was unchanged. Clothes still hung in the closets, and the drawers were full of the things of people who no longer lived here.

Standing in the den, I looked out over the backyard, across the gulley in front of the electrical plant and onto the small hills that rolled up to an open sky that was stretched into sapphire, streaked with the trails of jets leaving Newark Airport. The jets made me think of escape, but I was trapped in the den with thoughts of my mother. This was where she died.

My mother despised doctors. Even after being diagnosed with serious heart disease, she refused to be hospitalized. She had no insurance, so she set up a bed in the den and sent for me in Louisiana. While I managed to get her to allow me to hire a private nurse who checked in on her once a day, I was the one who took care of her. I helped her bathe, changed her bedpans and fed her soup spiked with black market morphine. Every night I slept on the floor by her side, my dreams racked with memories of coming home from school in the middle of the afternoon to find my mother between shifts at the diner, preparing dinner for us. The air smoked with aroma as sauce bubbled on the stove, my mother asleep on the couch, a cigarette burning in an ashtray on the coffee table. I'd blow roses in her thick hair until she opened her eyes and smiled. "Come," she'd say, rising slowly and taking me by the hand to the kitchen.

Tucked up against her side in front of the counter, my cheeks pressed against her polyester uniform, I watched as her dark, swollen hands turned eggs in a mound of flour, the sun shining in through the paned window. She'd then roll the dough out across the kitchen counter and cut it into ribbons which she would drop right into the steaming sauce. Leaving a swath of flour on my chin as she kissed my forehead, she'd tell me to eat before the others got home. Then she'd go smoke another cigarette and freshen up before returning to work the late shift.

My mother had many painful episodes on the road to death, excruciating moments where she wheezed and coughed, sucked for air like a fish caught in dirt. During those attacks, I often thought of putting a pillow to her face, but I never could build up the nerve. One night right before the end, after a particular bad episode, she shared the story of our family. "Listen," she rasped, as she told me that her mother had actually found the man she came to America to kill, found him in New Orleans. He worked on the water as a boat captain and lived in the Garden District with his wife and young son. My grandmother silently stalked the man every day, learning his habits, studying his dust. From the street she would watch through the window as he and his wife and their young child ate dinner by the golden light of dusk. After dinner, he would take a walk on the cobblestone streets, where he'd smoke and whistle to the night, counting his blessings from God, the blessings of America. She killed him on one of those walks, in the shadow of an alleyway. Split him like an Easter lamb, then watched him bleed out. When he was dead, she cleaned her knife on his shirt, spat on the ground, and left that night for New York.

My mother's mother had told my mother all this at the height of her dementia, sitting in the same metal chair where she had passed her days carving slivers of raw garlic with her stiletto and taunting her husband and daughter with tales of regret and revenge. That very night, after hearing the story of the murder, my mother kissed her father goodbye and hopped on the orphan's motorcycle. It was the last thing her mother had said to her, and was the last thing my mother said to me before she died. The end of the story, according to her. But I knew that there was more.

The murder had been reported as a robbery, the culprit never found. Afraid for their safety, the widow of the dead man moved to the backwoods with her son. The boy grew up without a father, a child of the Bayou. He eventually married a Creole woman, and they had a daughter named Carmen with corkscrew hair and green apple eyes who would one day fall in love with a traveler named Caesar Stiles. Carmen's father had told me this the night before I left for home to care for my sick mother, sitting in a rocking chair on his front porch, a shotgun across his lap, unaware of my true identity and the fantastic reality that my grandmother had murdered his father. While neither he nor I knew the whole story that night, he told me never to return, as travelers were not to be trusted.

**

The sky was the color of salmon when I left the house to walk into town. The traffic along the road had increased with the activity of the evening rush, and I felt the eyes of my hometown glance at me as cars slowed for a moment and people looked at me before speeding away from what to them was an unfamiliar face. A desire to be seen, to be recognized, surged inside of me. I was tired of being a stranger.

There was time to kill before the next train back to the city, so I decided to eat dinner at the inn, to find out for myself what all the complaining was about. I had never actually been inside the place, though I had peeked through the small, slotted windows many times as a kid, hoping to spot my father when I saw his motorcycle parked by the curb outside. The view through the dirty windows had always been hazy, and I'd never gotten a true sense of the room.

Entering the inn for the first time, I noticed how little light there was, even in the twilight of daytime. The room was split in half, with a bar, booths and small tables on one side, and an open dining room on the other. The walls were covered in wood paneling, reminding me of an old train depot. I sat at the bar.

The bartender was a man in his fifties with soft-white hair pushed back around the sides of his head. He wore a white shirt with black pants; a red apron tied tight around his paunch. He had sparkling blue eyes and an easy smile.

"What can I get ya'?" he asked, leaning into the bar with both hands, a clean towel over his shoulder, his voice still holding the hard scrabble of the Bronx. Except for two old men at a back table watching the TV bolted to the wall above the bar, I was the only person in the joint. I ordered a pint of Guinness and a steak sandwich, medium rare. The bartender wrote the order on a ticket, stuck it on a nail at the waiter's station and rang a desk bell. A bus boy immediately came through the swinging kitchen door, grabbed the ticket and returned to the kitchen.

The bartender spun a pint glass once around his palm and angled it under the Guinness tap. The effervescence roiled into the bottom of the glass as a deep brown rose on top of itself with a thin beige head. It was a tough drink to pour, but he handled it like an old pro. Behind him, the bar was in perfect order, everything polished to a high shine. There were no neon beer signs obstructing the mirror—no advertisements at all as a matter of fact. All the bottles were arranged neatly, the stacked glasses in easy reach.

"Done that before?" I asked the bartender.

"Once or twice," he said with a wink.

He put the glass in front of me then walked away. I took a sip—the stout tasted of burnt chocolate—as I considered the room. It had potential, though more seats and better light were needed. Ditching the train motif was probably a good idea, too, as was fixing the jukebox in the nook at the front of the bar. However, the actual bar itself was in good shape and the 'tender couldn't have been better. After a few minutes he came back, placed the steak sandwich in front of me and refilled my glass without my having to ask.

"It's on me," he said.

I didn't like that. While it might be good for tips, putting a customer's second drink on the house was bad for business. Free rounds had to be earned. But when I tasted the sandwich, I understood the bartender's generosity—he needed to make a living, and the food was a disaster. First off, the steak was the wrong cut—sirloin instead of flank or hangar—and had been overcooked. While the long roll was a decent choice, it had been over-toasted and buried with burnt garlic. A simple scratching with a raw clove is all you need to make garlic bread, as opposed to filling someone's mouth with instant halitosis. The sandwich also needed red onions and mayonnaise, not pickles and Russian dressing, and the onion rings had been fried in old oil, vegetable at that, instead of peanut oil.

I took a few more reluctant bites, before finally pushing away my plate. The bartender walked over slowly. "Would you like to take the rest of this home?" he asked with exaggerated formality.

"That's all right," I said. "I don't have a dog."

He laughed out loud and picked up the plate and carried it down to the waiter's station at the end of the bar. From down there, he crossed his arms and stared at me as I finished my stout. Not particularly good manners, I thought, for a bartender with particularly good manners. I set my eyes on him.

"Help you with something?" I asked.

"I'm sorry," he said, "but I've been thinking about something since you walked in here, and I gotta ask. You're Tim Stiles' kid, ain't ya'?"

I felt the floor move beneath me. My face flashed with heat. I couldn't help but look away.

The bartender laughed. "I knew it," he said. "I never forget a face and yours has had me going since you walked in. You look just like him, you know. Just darker and, you know, bigger."

"You don't say," I said, the world sort of spinning around me.

He walked over. "That's right," he said. "He used to sit right there where you're sitting now. Right in the middle of the room so everyone could hear him tell his stories." His reverie then fell silent as I imagined him recalling what happened when my father's stories went on for too long. I wondered how many times this bartender had thrown my father out of this place.

"You're not meeting him here today, are you?" the bartender asked.

"And how in the fuck would I meet him here?" I hadn't meant to say it like that, but it was out there now and I couldn't take it back.

"Hey," he said, holding up his hands. "He does drop in occasion, you know."

"What?" I asked as if I'd just been hit between the eyes with a pool ball. I hadn't heard a word from my father in thirteen years. I figured he was dead or out west, as far as the road would take him. Even the orange man couldn't find him. Yet now I was hearing that he still drank at his old bar, in his old town.

"That's right," the bartender said. "A few years back he dropped in one day out of the blue. Said he was living in a cabin he had built out by the Delaware Water Gap. I hadn't seen him in years. He looked the same, though. Must be good genes or something. He still comes by once and while for a few pops. He was just in here, I don't know, about a month ago." The bartender continued talking, but I couldn't hear what he was saying, as my ears were full of static. I stepped carefully off the bar stool as if I'd been on it for hours, left a twenty dollar tip on a fifteen dollar tab, and walked out the door.

Stumbling onto the sidewalk, I lit a cigarette. Faint darkness had been drawn like a shade. I walked across the street in a cloud of confusion, my head swimming with thoughts about my father. What did he know about his ravaged family? Was he here for the house? Why hadn't he come looking for me? Maybe he had. I kept coming back to that last thought—maybe my father was looking for me?

"Hey," someone suddenly called out in a raspy voice. I was snapped from my thoughts as if I'd been bashed across the knees with a baseball bat as Sallie stomped across the repair shop's lot. He had his shirt off and was using it to rub grease from his hands. Chin high and chest out, he approached with feigned curiosity, even a hint of delight.

"What are you doing out here, C?"

"Came for a beer," I mumbled.

"Where? There?" he said, pointing across the street. "Nobody goes there no more. The place is filled with fucking yuppies."

"Okay," I said, having trouble coming up with words, still stunned by what the bartender had told me about my father.

"So what else you come out here for?" Sallie asked, fluttering up his chin. "The house, right?"

"Right," I said.

As my brother crossed his arms, his chest and shoulders barreled. He reminded me of a rhino. The muscles around his mouth and jaws twitched. "Good thinking, C," he said nodding. "Good thinking." He seemed pleased, and his vibrancy pulsed like a power line.

Crossing car lights flashed over us as Sallie threw his greasy shirt in a trash can. "Huey gave me my job back," he said. "Let's me sleep upstairs in the office."

"That's good," I said.

"Yeah, for the time being," Sallie said. "Know what I mean?" He looked practically giddy and I almost thought he was going to ask me out for a beer. Instead, he nodded at the cigarette pack sticking out of my jeans. I extended the pack, and he took two smokes, put one behind his ear, tore the filter off the other and threw it on the ground. He flicked open a Zippo and hit the flame.

"You know how it is with me C," he said, "I got my way of doing things, seeing things. My way. I don't give a fuck what some lawyer says or what some town says. I know what's right. I know what's mine. That house is mine, C. It belongs to me. I fucking earned it." Sallie blew smoke over his shoulder and took a deep breath. A car honked for service at the gas pump, but my brother didn't budge, his face tangled from the strain of communication.

"You don't even know," he continued. "I'm the one who Pop kicked around all the time, the one who bled all over that house and all over that yard. And I'm the one who built himself up and ran that fucker off. You should be grateful, C. I saved your ass," he laughed. "I'm not gonna lie here and say I did it for you. I never liked you, you know that. But, still, me running Pop off saved you scars, man. I'll fucking tell you that. So, the way I see it, that house is mine. Make sense?"

"Sure," I said, though I knew my father would never hurt me. While he made life brutal, at times, for all of us, yelling and smashing and breaking things, all the physical stuff had always been between him and Sallie. The rest of us had been left out of it—until there was only one of them left. And now I knew that

Sallie was to blame for that.

"That's smart, C," Sallie said. "Even fucking Steven." He flicked the cigarette in the street and spit some tobacco flakes towards my boots. "See you tomorrow," he said, walking back to work, cackling. "At *your* house, in spooktown."

**

I waited on a bench at the depot, watching the moon rise over the tree line above the valley. I don't know how much time passed before the train whistle blew and the crossing gates went down as a black locomotive pulled a trail of shiny silver cars into the station. I boarded the last car. It was nearly empty, and I lied down like a little boy, on my side across two seats with my knees tucked in, my hands together in prayer for a pillow.

The train hissed and chugged then rolled in steady rhythm down the tracks as I remembered the way my father used to tassel my hair when I was a kid. How he'd twist the crown into a little nest, then squat down to my level and poke a finger gently into my chest. "And what's your story?" he'd ask, his eyes green and bright. I wouldn't talk. "No story today, huh?" he'd say. "Well, I've got one for you then." And he'd tell me something fantastic about an Irish boxer named J.L. Sullivan who knocked out ten men in one night, or the barmaid from Galloway with hair of black and eyes of blue who could end any feud with a glass of whiskey and a dance around the room. My favorite, however, was about Finn McCool, the gentle giant who lived with his lovely wife atop Knockmany Hill and defeated another giant by biting off his magic finger.

When he wasn't telling stories, my father would sing songs, or recite poems with words that floated in front of my face like butterflies. Sometimes, he'd make things up out of thin air, like when I'd sit on his lap and trace the scars above his eyes and under his hair and behind his ears and ask him where they had come from.

I'd hear those stories and songs and poems in my head during the nights I'd hide under the bed when my father came home pissed. Even after he was gone, I never found out why he drank so much, or what had happened to him in that orphanage in the Bronx. What made him suffer so much. All I knew was that it was deep and cruel and something he could never get past, no matter how many stories he told or songs he sang or poems he recited. No matter how many times his little boy sat on his lap, starring up at him with a look of wonder on his face.

**

The train pulled into at Penn Station. The doors slid open, and I walked into the late night caverns of the station. It was cold and unusually quiet, absent the chaos of commuters and tourists. A handful of people, dressed casually, were catching trains going in the opposite direction, heading out of town for the holiday weekend.

I took the subway down the east side of Manhattan, getting out at City Hall. As night sifted down in steady streams, I walked across the Brooklyn Bridge. Bathed in bright lights, the brilliant design of stone and cement held in place by suspension cables, like elegant drapes, it felt like the most important place in the world. It had taken thousands of men thirteen years to carve the granite stones and plant the cement beams into the murky base of the East River. I thought about one of those men—my mother's great grandfather—as I walked the bridge.

I'd looked him up on Ellis Island once, but all it said of Carmello Maccarone was that he'd arrived from Naples in 1870, the year the project had begun. I never found out exactly what he had done on the bridge, but in my mind, he was a master stone cutter, a short, dark man with large hands that swung as he walked. I imagined him, dusted in granite, eating his lunch on the bluffs along the Brooklyn side, watching his life's work materialize before his eyes. When the bridge was complete, I thought of him standing in the same spot where I stood now, on a broad landing, a huge American flag flying overhead.

The full moon rose above the harbor as brightly lit tour boats skimmed along the black water, the brilliant cluster of lower Manhattan piled like stacks of coins from a treasure chest in the distance. Up the river, bridges arched across the wide water all the way up the east side, while the Brooklyn side was marked by soft, round lights, like a string of pearls. Headlights and taillights streaked across the expressway under the promenade. As I got closer, shapes appeared in apartment windows. It reminded me of the painting by Jean-Baptist Rennet—the various symbols of home in the lighted windows of a townhouse, the spangle of the Brooklyn Bridge in the distance. Standing there amidst the wind and sky and lights, I finally recognized the artistic quality that made Jean-Baptist special: he understood what it meant to be home.

I squinted against the wind while descending the wood-planked walkway into Brooklyn. Lovers and bike riders passed. The roadway roared, then grew quiet underneath the landing. The underpass smelled of urine. I hurried out into the clean night air, feeling invisible in the darkened city. No one noticed me passing through the main avenues and side streets, past conversations and laughter. Things grew silent until the faint sound of music, static and unmelodious, came scratching down the empty streets. Falling through the trees, it washed over me like burning rain. I wandered off towards the music, which was coming from the direction of the art institute.

Across from campus, next to a closed diner, an unattached

frame house glowed with pale light on an otherwise desolate row of neglected homes. Figures spilled onto the rickety porch and hung out the second story window, their voices constant and mingled into an indecipherable murmur. A couch in the front yard was occupied like a floating vessel. Along the side, silhouettes filled the alley with postures of urination. The music was a fusion of ska and punk. I ducked through the doorway into the dim front room.

The furniture had been removed, replaced by beer puddles on the wooden floor. Faces were in shadows, in small groups under the low ceiling or staggered on the stairs, smoking and talking and drinking from small plastic cups or large bottles. Smoke drifted and voices climbed and fell from artists practicing their nonchalance. Heads bobbed but no one danced. Someone elbowed me in the back as they lurched past. I followed the low and dark familiar figure as she glided through the crowd. In the hallway, she walked into a narrow door without knocking. I inserted my boot before it slammed, slipped in during the rebound, and closed it quietly behind. I turned on the bathroom light.

The uncovered bulb blared from a cord. My gloomy friend covered her eyes and stared up at me. She scoffed, pulled down her tights, and sat on the toilet. A hissing sound came from between her legs. She stared absently ahead. When the hissing stopped, she took a square of toilet paper and wiped herself on both sides. She dropped it between her legs but didn't flush. "You got twenty bucks?" she asked me from the toilet seat, her pants still down.

"What?"

"I'll suck your dick," she said mechanically.

The glare from the bulb felt hot on my scalp. "No, thanks," I said.

"Then what the fuck do you want?" She looked up at me. Her face, in the brutal light, looked wan and sickly. Her lips were strips of picked skin over patches of dried blood. A sore blossomed beneath her nostrils. She pulled up her pants and tried to brush past me. I blocked her way. Her eyes went feral and she screeched inhumanely. Her teeth were stained and sharp along the side of her mouth. "Suck my bloody cunt," she blurted and tried to fight her way past. I didn't move, though I really wanted to get away. Instead I pushed her, harder than I meant to, and she fell back onto the toilet seat.

She laughed and asked coquettishly if I wanted to beat her up. "Come on," she purred. "It'll be fun."

"Where's JB?" I asked.

Her face changed expression again. "It doesn't matter," she said.

"And why's that?"

"Because nothing matters. Everything is bullshit. This school is bullshit. This party is bullshit. Art is bullshit. You're bullshit. He's bullshit. That freckled bitch is bullshit. The world is bullshit."

"Why don't you kill yourself?" I asked.

She pushed up her sleeves. She had scars of different depths and tones up both wrists, along with some serious burns. "Tried that," she said. "Never worked. I might be immortal."

"Too bad," I said.

"Yeah," she laughed. "But it's tolerable to just get high or feel pain. And maybe I'll kill somebody else along the way."

"You trying to kill JB?"

"Well, not directly," she said, perking up. "But I'm showing him how to do it."

"And does he want to die?" I asked her.

She scoffed. "No. He wants to suffer. He thinks his art won't be anything until her learns how to suffer like all those junkie musicians he likes so much. Or like Basquiat. You know, the dead fucking artists. He wants to be a suffering American nigger. He talks about it all the time. Fucking idiot. That's why he came here and why he lives where he lives and does what he does. So cool. The funny thing is, I think he got what he wanted. He's a fucking broke-ass nigger whose gonna die soon." She straightened on the toilet seat. "I'm really happy for him."

She began to cackle in that horrific way of hers. I left her behind and walked out of the bathroom and into the party. She followed me through the crowd and out the open door onto the porch, laughing the entire time. She pushed at my back as I went down the stairs and taunted me as I crossed the yard. The whole party watched. People withdrew into the shadows and stared.

I started up the block, but she was still on me, spewing invective. She finally went silent as we joined a desolate street without light and slipped under the long, deep shadows of a stretch of London Planes. She never came out the other end.

**

I was nearly home when the youngest boy from across the street rode by on his bicycle. He clacked past, probably not even noticing me in the shadows. He swerved down the middle of the road, whistling without care as he passed our corner and turned up the next. I thought about how much time he spent out in the middle of the night, and how he told me that he knew about Jean-Baptist. I ran down the street to the next corner and caught sight of him walking his bike through a vacant lot on the block behind his house.

I found a pay phone and called Don, but got no answer. It was late on a Friday night, so he was probably knee-deep in great big ass. I left a message, told him what I had in mind. The wind was whipping, and my eyes and nose filled with dust as I walked the desolate block behind mine, a barren one way with gutted brownstones and low-slung brick apartment houses. My boots pulverized broken vials on the cracked sidewalk. In the empty lot behind the boy's house, through the plunging tree branches, a light was visible upstairs, but any sound was muted by the wind that flayed the chain link fence and rattled the branches.

A trail scored the knee-high weeds. A kick of the fence, where the trail commenced, revealed a clipped slit. Almost through the divided metal, my hood snagged on one of the protruding fragments, preventing me from getting caught in the car lights that flashed across the yard. I rolled into the overgrowth as the lights went out, listening in the weeds to the engine idle on the other side of the fence.

Slowly, I crawled on my hands and knees behind a tree. A figure, stealth and feral, scurried across the trail and through the fence without pause. The rattling sound of the car increased as the window lowered and then quietly closed. In the pale light, I watched the young boy go back inside.

The wind pushed the branches down and shook the gutter that dangled off the back of the house. I crept up to the pained back door and looked through the window. Two figures on the far side of the room lounged in the pale light of a flickering TV. The young boy was in front, his silhouette obvious enough. I couldn't make out the second figure. On a trunk in front of them, unknown objects reflected in the blue light. The front room appeared to be the kitchen, though there were no appliances, just crumbled bags and containers discarded over the floor and countertops. A stairwell, in the center of the ground floor, separated the small apartment from a room from where I could hear and feel the boiler roaring.

Back in the far side of the room, the objects from the trunk were put into action: a flame rose before being sucked into the end of a pipe. Smoke flitted across the TV screen. The pipe was passed back and forth. After the pipe returned to the make-shift tabletop, the figures slumped into the couch. A harsh, stale scent leaked out the window as a squealing sound approached through the whispering wind.

I looked over to see the silent man leave his cart by the side-walk, then barge through the fence and through the overgrown backyard. I folded into a shadow against the side of the house as he stooped through the yard and in through the back door. A light went on and glowed against the glass of the kitchen win-dow. The silent man's voice rose in a rage. "What I tell you!" he boomed. "What I tell you!"

I went to the window and watched him drag the young boy off the couch. Left there alone on the sofa, Jean-Baptist, his face now clear in the overhead light, reared back against the wall. He wore a mask of panic. The silent man shook the little boy by the shirt collar, a bag of bones in the big man's grip. "What I tell you!" he screamed right in the boy's face. Then he hurled him across the room, spilling him across the kitchen floor like a glass of milk. The boy lay in a crumpled heap under my eyes in the window. I pulled the knife I always carried out of my pants. The silent man approached the boy again as I slipped through the door. When I got to the kitchen threshold, the little boy was being lifted off his feet.

"Come on, now" I said reasonably with my knife in one hand and my other hand out to the side. "You don't have to hurt him like that." My heart was thumping and my clothes began to moisten. My hair felt heavy on my shoulders.

The silent man studied me like I was an apparition, as if he couldn't trust his own eyes. He released the boy, who scurried into the darkness. "What you want here?" he asked, still stunned by my presence. There was a glint of genuine worry in his eye. He looked for the boy, then back to me. No one spoke. Heavy breathing filled the air. I realized then that the silent man was the reason the older boys left that younger one alone. He was his protector—an Angie to their duo of Sallies. The man and the boy must live down there in the bottom of the house that they entered from the back, on a separate block, in a separate world. The boy must have befriended JB during his desperate search for drugs and brought him home. And now here I was in their world, facing down a wild man worried about his sort-of-son.

Before anyone had a chance to do anything else, the boy came at me low and from the side, stealth-like from out of the darkness, with a small blade, probably a razor. It swept my side as fast as it appeared, slicing through my sweatshirt and thermal and splitting the skin below my ribs. I crumpled over in a protective reflex, succumbing to the stinging and the burn, then hit the floor. Two sets of feet scurried over and around me, then out the back door. JB and the boy, I assumed. Before I could get to one knee, a mighty fist caught me in the temple and sent me to the floor again. The smell of basement filled my nose as black washed over me.

I was in the Mediterranean, floating in the warm water of my ancestors. I rose and fell in the hard green sea, salt in my nose and sun on my face, my fanned hair like a cape behind me. Fishing boats were moored to a nearby jetty, and brilliant white birds circled in the swimming pool sky. Across a piazza beyond the sand, an olive-skinned woman appeared in the window of a white-washed villa, an apron tied over the hem of her billowing blouse. She raised a hand to me, and I swam for the shore, but the tugging sea wouldn't let me advance. I swam and swam, but the tide took me out as the birds overhead began to circle and scream. My lungs began to seize. I stopped fighting.

Warm liquid interrupted my dream. I opened my eyes. Urine crossed my cheek and entered my mouth. Above me, Pimples held his dick and cackled just out of reach, while High Fade muttered "Oh, shit!" over and over again. I'd been moved to the sofa, and sat there paralyzed in the bright light as Pimple's piss receded down my torso and across my knee. He shook the remnants on my boot.

"How you like that motherfucker," he howled, leaning in towards me as he spoke. "Coming into our house and shit. Man, you must be fucking crazy!" High Fade kicked me hard under the kneecap. The boys looked stoned, in oversized sweatshirts and jeans, slant-eyed in the middle of the night. The silent man and the youngest boy were gone. It was just me and Pimples and High Fade amidst the exposed pipes and detritus of a decrepit basement.

I moaned. They laughed. An octopus of pain sucked on my head. All my senses were engaged in discomfort. I passed out again. I don't believe I was out for long before Cyrus's slaps woke me up. He leaned over the couch; I could smell his sleep-stink breath. His voice echoed in my ringing ears. "Get up, man. Get up!" He slapped away until I opened my eyes. The silent man was now behind him and the two older boys leaned against the wall, cross-armed with surly looks on their faces.

"Help me out here, Sean," Cyrus said. The silent man came over. Sean. I would have laughed at such a common name had I had the strength. The two men lifted me by the elbows and began leading me across the room towards the back door. My knife was on the ground against the near wall.

"The hell you going?" High Fade asked from behind in a condescending and aggressive tone.

Our progress stopped. Cyrus turned his head to the side. "Who are you talking to like that?" he asked with authority. He faced the boys; Sean and I turned with him.

"I'm talking to you, old man," High Fade said with disgust. "That fucking white boy just walk in here on his own, and you gonna let him walk out? Hell, no." He and Pimples stared at Cyrus, their chins high, their eyes slanted with defiance.

"Well, you boys must be crazy," Cyrus said, his grip tightening on my elbow as his chest fell and rose. "This here is *my* house, and I sure as hell won't be disrespected like that."

"Shit," High Fade spat. "The fuck you know about respect? You ain't do shit around here except collect them checks. This is our house and we ain't letting that white bitch go."

"Now listen here," Cyrus barked.

But before he could offer his decree, Pimples reached behind to his waistband and pulled out a dull gray pistol. It glimmered in the basement light as he pointed it at Cyrus' face. The silent man staggered next to me.

"Here's how it gonna go," High Fade announced. "We gonna kill this white bitch and leave his ass up there by the school. Hang him on that big fence they got." He pointed at Cyrus and Sean, directed them over to the back by the couch. I moved against the far wall as the boys rotated over and faced me with their back to the darkened stairwell. The gun was held on me but the conversation was pointed at Cyrus. "And then we ain't gonna have to worry about no more of this gentrification shit you always talking to us about. Got it, Coach? You fired. You won't have to take this crazy fucker off his meds so he can scare people away. We won't have to get hassled by them cops for selling our shit in the daylight. No more bullshit. We done tried it your way and look what we got—white boys across the street, disrespecting us and shit. We'll kill this white motherfucker and them property people be gone for a long time. Hell, they probably close the whole damn school down, too. And all you gotta do, fat man, is shut the fuck up and stay out our way or we be coming for yo' ass next. This here our house now, our neighborhood now. Understand motherfucker?"

Both boys chuckled and nodded with pride. Cyrus slumped, failure freighting his shoulders. In the silence, Pimples' face grew serious and his grip tightened on the gun. He sneered and breathed through his nose. His mouth twitched. He clicked the hammer back. I closed my eyes, too beat up and tired to worry about dying. Imaginary trains whipped past, and I felt my hair rise and fall. I waited, but nothing happened. Then something thudded off the floor. A tisking sound came from the stairwell, behind the boys. I opened my eyes. The dull gray pistol was on the ground. High Fade and Pimples stood dead still, looking younger than they had a moment before, separate gun barrels inches behind their heads.

"Oh, Caesar," Don sang, hunched on the stairs. "Told you to be careful with these gangsters."

He slipped down the stairs, kicked Pimples' gun into the center of the room then stepped around the boys, his barrels still trained on them, his overcoat opened like a cape, his hair and face covered in white panty hose. He picked up the gun off the floor and sidled up to me. He bobbed his head with a sneer evident through the nylon, double-cocked both hammers and pointed them at the boys. I imagined, under the mask, his pupils blooming like night flowers.

"Which one of y'all pissed on my partner?"

With his eyes, High Fade sold out Pimples, who looked at the floor. Don shot him through the foot. The explosion made the tiles explode off the ground. The boy hopped around screaming. Pieces of his sneaker and foot were splattered low on the wall. When his hopping led him towards the center of the room, Don butted him in the mouth with the gun handle. Pimples fell to the floor, bleeding from his head and foot. A puddle of blood began to form on the corroded ceramic.

Don looked down at the bleeding boy. "Need quiet," he said, but Pimples kept wailing. Don said it again, this time with the hammer cocked in the direction High Fade's face.

"Quiet, motherfucker," High Fade seethed, kicking his foster brother in the side. Pimples began a keening whimper as he shuddered on the ground. Tears poured down his face as he continued to quietly sob.

Don studied the older one, squinting into his eyes. "Ready to die?" he asked.

High Fade raised his chin. Don fired a shot through his hair. The bullet lodged in the wall behind him. Don asked High Fade again if he was ready to die. The boy shook his head, fear and gun powder all over his face. Blood began to leak from his ear.

"You know who I am?" Don asked.

High Fade nodded.

"Say my name."

"Mr. Brown," he mumbled.

Don studied him for a moment, letting the silence and the threat sink into the boy's psyche.

"All right," Don finally said, lowering his guns abruptly. "You don't know me, or where I stay, or nothing; but I know you, I know you good, and I'll come by sometime soon, maybe tomorrow, and if I see you, it too late." He raised his guns back up. "Understand what I say?"

High Fade nodded.

"And I know who you work for over there on that corner, that man named Broadous with the Range Rover and I know where that Range Rover park at night over on Aimsley, and if something happen to my partner or my partner's house or my partner's sidewalk even, I'll be putting your boss on the top of my list. I be sending word to Broadous that he free from Mr. Brown as long as he partner be let alone." Don touched the barrel of a gun to the boy's temple, "*Tink* about it."

He raised his guns again, aiming one on Cyrus. "What about him," Don asked me. "What the fat man have to do with this?"

I wanted to say he had everything to do with it, using those kids like he did, but I was afraid it might get him shot. Besides, Cyrus had already been defeated.

"Nothing," I said. "Let's go."

Don cleared a path for us and motioned for me to head up the stairs. He followed behind, walking backwards with his guns up. My knife lay in the corner, against the sideboards. I pocketed it then limped up the stairs.

Don and I walked through the desolate parlor and out into the glowing night. We crossed through the yard and past the Continental that rusted in the moist air. Don turned up the collar of his overcoat and peeled off his mask. Dropping it at his side, he disappeared down the middle of the street. "I'll be seeing ya, Caesar," he said with his back to me.

I stumbled up the stairs to my house. Once inside, I stripped off my clothes and tended to my wounds. It could have been worse. I could have been crucified, hung from the fence of the art institute. An ironic martyr, as I stood for nothing.

After bandaging myself, I limped upstairs, lay down on my bed and succumbed to exhaustion and the delicious breath of life.

**

I dreamed that I was a little boy, sitting on the stoop of my house in Brooklyn, waiting, until the faint sound of a motorcycle tickles my ear. It grows closer and louder, until my father takes the corner in a slow, sweeping turn. The wind stands up the collar of his sleeveless jean jacket and the buttons bounce of his bare chest. His hair is bent back by the breeze. He parks his bike in front of the house and takes his time getting off.

He looks just like the last time I saw him: lean and raw, with terse muscles and loose eyes. He looks at me and smiles warmly. His boots trace my sidewalk and echo as they climb the wooden stairs. He nods towards the door. We go inside. He inspects the beveled glass of the antique mirror in the hall. In the open parlor he admires the restored floors and uses his eyes, below the high ceiling, to trace the contours of the hand-carved frieze. He nods and walks through the house with his head on a swivel. Everything makes him happy. Then he kneels down and takes my hands, my grown up hands, the hands I have now. He fingers the calluses and scars, studies the veins that rise defiantly on the back. He tassels my hair into a bird's nest and kisses my forehead. And then he disappears, the moisture from his lips still wet on my skin.

# *Saturday*

Lillian Pettaway was busy ringing up lottery tickets for a khaki-colored girl who had a hand on one hip and a child in the other. The girl had on a tight, faded tank top showing a lot of bone in her arms, shoulders and upper back. With her free hand, she reached up and patted a handkerchief on her head while rattling off numbers in a mechanical fashion. From behind the glass, Ms. Pettaway looked up over her spectacles at me.

"Didn't figure to see you again," she said before returning her gaze to the machine as it cranked out a long trail that snaked onto the counter and buckled into a stack.

"And why's that?" I asked.

"That French boy been back two days now. Him and freckles been coming and going like flies."

"They up there now?"

"Can't say for sure. Just opened."

The machine stopped. The girl dropped a wad of cash into the belly of the partition. Ms. Pettaway looked at the cash, then at the girl. She let her glasses drop to her bosom and stared until the girl shifted her hips and asked, "What?"

"Why don't you take that money and go buy her a dollie or something?"

"Look," the girl answered fiercely, "I ain't got no time today for none of yo' shit. You want the money or not? I'll go down to the Jews to buy my tickets. I don't give no fuck."

Ms. Pettaway sighed, put her glasses back on, and collected the cash. She counted it slowly before finally handing over the tickets through the partition and watching sadly as the too-skinny girl with a baby on her hip did a lazy sway into the morning light. Below Ms. Pettaway's eye, a wrinkle twitched into the puffed flesh. She looked at me and I looked back, both of us recognizing our mutual understanding of what it meant to be weary.

"What happened to you?" she asked, taking notice of the swelling around my temple and the dark circles around my eyes.

"Long night," I said.

"I can see," she said, nodding with resignation. "Miss Lillian can't help you with that."

"I know," I said. "But I was hoping to ask you a few questions."

"About what?"

"About Montgomery Davis and Claire Horton."

"We'll, Goddamn," she said, smacking the counter. "Ain't you just a regular Easy Rawlins."

"Hardly," I said.

She smiled. I pointed toward a bottle, but she held up her hand.

"Ah, hell, you caught me in a talking mood today anyway."

She invited me behind the glass, and while sharing a smoke under the reflection of the liquor bottles, Ms. Lillian Pettaway told me the story of the neighborhood where she'd lived since she was a baby girl. She told me how, during and after segregation, families came up from the Carolinas in search of milk and honey, and how they found it in the steady work of the navy yard and the factories. Back then, the neighborhood was safe and respectable. Everybody knew everybody. Daddies, carrying lunchboxes, walked their little boys and girls to school.

Then the navy yard closed. The factories followed. The

daddies disappeared and welfare arrived. Milk and honey turned into malt liquor. The boys without fathers sold drugs on the once safe streets and got fatherless girls pregnant, creating a generation of lost children that lived down the slope and throughout the flats. She said it had been getting worse with the passing years. Now they shoot each other over nothing, play their music as loud as they want and curse people out. All of them dressed like hoodlums and whores. Don't have respect for nothing. She said it was like a prison around here now—no one ever gets out. Trapped, she said. They're all trapped.

She'd been brought up with Montgomery Davis and Claire Horton. Said they were good boys from good families. Montgomery's dad had been the local dentist and Claire's owned the bar across from the navy yard. He'd moved that bar up to the heights after the factories closed, to make his money off them uppity Negroes. Eventually, the dentist and the barman got themselves into the property business and ended up owning half the damn neighborhood. Still, they were fair about the rent and loaned money at a rate people could afford, not like them bloodsuckers over at the bank.

Then the dentist retired and the bar owner died of a heart attack right on the floor of his joint the night before Easter, forty years ago this very day. The two men's sons then took over, got themselves incorporated and everything. Claire ran the bar, Montgomery watched the money. Neither of them ever married, too busy with business and young women. One of them girls claimed to have a baby by Claire, a boy called Cyrus. Nobody believed her since the boy didn't look nothing like a Horton, but Claire took some responsibility anyway. He gave the lady and her boy free rent and some money each month, but the rub was that the boy could never call him daddy. The mother eventually had another baby by another father, and that boy wasn't right from jump street. He'd go from silent to stormy in the drop of a hat. And he just got worse as he came up. Got all mixed up in them drugs, too.

Claire gave that boy and his brother Cyrus some work once it was clear they weren't going nowhere on they own. He had them collect rent and debts, though sometimes they went too far. They didn't have that touch with people that Claire and Montgomery had. People started to complain, but Claire didn't do nothing about it. He let that Cyrus boy go on his own. And now he go around like he King Shit. Let them buildings go down. Has his hands into other things, too. Got a bunch of them foster kids he making money off. Has them set up two, three to a house. Think he slick taking dimes from the city. But that kind of shit come home to roost. And it might just be coming soon. This proper Negro that looked like a young Billy Dee had come in offering a near mint for her building. Told her straight up that the college was expanding, and housing would be at a premium, and that more and more people were leaving the city and moving out to Brooklyn. Why they'd want to come round here, she had no idea.

I asked her if she believed that the neighborhood was really changing for the better. She said she didn't know. "We still got a lot of problems around here," she said, looking out at the streets, where a group of sulking young men had gathered silently on the corner. "Like I said, it's more like a prison here than a neighborhood. I didn't think it could get any worse, but I believe it has. God knows what's coming next." She stared out at the boys on the street. "At least I don't take no stamps and I do what I can to keep my building safe. We'll just have to wait and see what happens 'round here."

"Speaking of this building," I said. "Is there a way I can get inside? I'd like to have a word with Freckles."

"I think that may be possible," she said, clutching my arm and smiling. "After all, I know the owner."

**

The carpeting moved under my feet in the empty corridor as I headed towards 4G. No one answered my knock. I tried the knob and the door opened. Inside, the small front room was poorly lit by an overhead light, its base filled with dead flies. Unframed canvases lie stacked around the room, and an easel in the corner held a work in progress. Light wafted in from the kitchen where Colette sat at a round table, staring at Jean-Baptist Rennet, who sat slouched in a folding chair. He was shirtless and unshaven, his mop of greasy brown hair pushed back off his pimpled forehead. He was like a bad looking version of his sister. Colette had on the same black sweater dress she'd worn the afternoon we'd met. Stretched and wrinkled, it hung on her like a sack. Her face was pale and drawn, her freckles gone to mud.

"Hello," I said.

Colette jumped up and rushed to me. "*Nicoise!*"

I held her away to protect my injured side.

"Please! Please!" she said. "I am happy to see you. I am happy to see you. I went to your home and..."

I showed her my bandaged flank.

"*Oh, Nicoise,*" she sighed. She rubbed my face with her fingers. "*Derangue.*"

I studied the kitchen. The sink was piled with dirty dishes, the counter a scatter of empty wine bottles and juice glasses sticky with purple at the bottom. The sunlight that peered through the small window failed to add sparkle to anything. The refrigerator door was open; the floor tiles curled up and stained. Rat droppings gathered in the corner. The kitchen table was a large wooden electrical spool turned on its side. The chairs around it were metal.

"I came here like you tell me," she said. "I come to tally paintings and bring one to the man at the school. But when I come, Jean is here. He is sick and he need help." She waved a hand at her comatose brother. "I'm sorry, *Nicoise*. Caesar. I try to help but I don't know how. I come to you, to find your help, but that man is in your house. He tell me not to come back. To stay away from you. When I come home, Jean is gone. But he return last night, very late. And very scared. He cry and cry. And then he sleep. Just like this."

"He needs to go home," I said to Colette.

"This is home," she said.

"To France," I said. "He needs to go home to France. You, too."

Colette looked at me sadly. I touched her shoulder as I pushed past to draw a glass of water from the sink, which I threw in Jean-Baptist's face. He jolted to attention, shaking his head. "What are you doing?" he snarled, wiping water from his eyes. He jumped up upon recognizing me, but I pushed him back down into his chair. I held an open hand, commanding him to stay put.

I walked into the front room, and returned a minute later holding one of his canvases.

"I'll give you two plane tickets for this painting." It was the painting from the postcard.

"What?" Jean-Baptist asked.

"You heard me," I said. "Pack up what you can carry. You're going home today."

Colette's sudden embrace felt like a knife in my side, but I let her stay there for awhile anyway.

\*\*

From the corner in front of Lilian Pettaway's building I hailed a cab, and together the three of us sailed away from the dirty avenue toward the airport. The cab, a low-riding town car in need of a new suspension system, squeaked and bounced as it absorbed every bump and hole of the BQE. We jockeyed through light traffic, past faded advertisements painted on the sides of buildings above bleak neighborhoods and industrial zones, yards of scrap metal and dormant delivery trucks, vast parking lots for school buses.

Colette sat in the middle, her eyes focused on the road ahead. Jean-Baptist had the window seat facing the city. He stared at the skyline, pewter in the daytime, like a mountain range of metal, as we zoomed across a little bridge and forked onto the highways of Queens, toward Kennedy Airport. As Manhattan disappeared behind us, Jean-Baptist turned to watch it vanish out the back window.

**

The airport was nearly empty. I bought two tickets at the Air France counter. The next available flight wasn't until six o'clock, and I hoped it took off on time. They'd arrive in Nice the following morning, and I imagined the South of France being a wonderful place to come home to.

From over my shoulder, Collette spoke rapid French to the ticket agent and tugged on Jean-Baptist's arm as he stared at his shoes or in the other direction. At some point, he'd have to reconcile the shame of what had happened to him in America if he wished to survive. He had to tear down the myth he'd made of himself. I'd have to do the same.

I told them both goodbye and took a taxi back to Brooklyn, my new painting next to me on the seat.

**

I ran a hot bath when I got home, soaking my wounds in isolation. Eventually, I drifted off to sleep in the warm water, and found myself with my childhood friends in the comfort of our boxed-in block. Sunlight shreds its way through the growing oak trees, making us squint as we try to follow the ball coming out of the pitcher's hand. A bashful girl watches us from her driveway, sitting on the ground with skinny arms around bare knees. A metal bat clatters off the concrete. Birds scatter as voices rise with the floating ball. The air is sweet, the sky blue and streaked with thin white clouds, the sun warm on our faces.

The moment gently breaks as the ball arches down and bounces across a yard. Bodies move in perfect motion as if choreographed. There are footsteps and calls. A relay is arranged as a runner circles the narrow diamond of trees and manhole covers. A throw is made, but the result doesn't matter. We start up again in the endless cycle of children at play. The day is ours as long as we want it. There are no demons or doubt, just kids at play on a dead end street, safe at home.

**

I awoke when the bathwater grew cold. I set fresh bandages and got dressed in jeans and boots and a hooded sweatshirt with loaded pockets. With my hair tucked into the back of the sweatshirt, I waited on the top of the stoop until Sallie came swaggering down the block sucking on a cigarette. He wore a tight black t-shirt and new biker boots. I pulled up the hood and dug my hands into the pockets.

"What do you say there, C?" Sallie said as he came up to my gate. His face wore an expectant and arrogant smirk.

"Not much," I answered.

"All right, then," he said, shrugging. "What do you got for me?"

"For you?"

He blew some air out of his nose. "You told me to be here. Here I am. I know you didn't ask me over to talk old times."

A black sedan with tinted windows slowly drove by as I walked down to the steps to the sidewalk. "I do have something for you," I said, and spit a huge gob of saliva in Sallie's face. He stepped back violently, his eyes wide and wild.

"You fucking suicidal?" he barked, wiping his face. "You wanna die?"

I stood there with my hands in my front pockets, fingering the items hidden within.

"I ain't here to play games with you," Sallie warned with a hard finger that poked me between the eyes. "I came for Ma's fucking house and I ain't leaving without it." He smelled of smoke, sweat and motor oil. "Act like a fucking tough guy if you want, but I'll stay right here on these steps for as long as it takes. You want that, C? You want to see me every fucking day? Take a beating every fucking day like you used to? Remember how many times I split your face open? Remember that, pussy? Those times I beat you cold?" He was right under my chin; his sour breath filled my nose. "How about when I shattered your ribs, or when I cut off your fucking homo hair? Yeah, I miss those times and I'm ready to relive them every fucking day 'til you give me what I came for. You know me, C."

"It's not Ma's house," I said, my hands still in my pockets.

He leaned his ear toward me. "What?"

"It's not Ma's house," I said, right into his ear. "It's mine. And you'll have to kill me to get it."

Right after the last word left my mouth, Sallie's fist slammed into my cheekbone, knocking me to the ground. I tasted dirt and blood as the sole of his boot stomped across my mouth. A busted tooth scratched at my throat as I rolled onto my back. Sallie then jumped on top of me, his repeated blows like cinder blocks dropping from the sky. I didn't try to wrestle free as I slipped my hands down and fished through the pockets of my sweatshirt, each punch feeling like an explosion against my face and body. Eventually, I entered into oblivion.

The wail of a siren returned me to consciousness. Footsteps rushed from up the street, from where the unmarked sedan was parked. Someone with authority called, "Hands! Hands! Hands! Goddamn it! Hands!" The punches stopped. Beneath the blurry sky, two guns were now aimed at my brother's head. His hands were open and in the air. "Now step off," the voice behind one gun said. "Slowly." The weight of my brother lifted off of me.

Sallie looked around, stunned and furious. "Who the fuck are you?" he demanded to know.

Will's giant cop friend ushered Sallie to my fence, where his partner, red-faced and equally large, cuffed my brother and began reading him his rights. Will knelt down next to me. "Goddamn, man!" he said. "You Okay, Stiles? Jesus. I ain't never seen no shit like that before."

Blood poured from my cheekbone. Bruises began to take shape all over my head. The world was slanted. I spit half a tooth on the ground. I felt light headed, as if time had been suspended. Neighborhood people started to gather on the sidewalk, their whispers inaudible.

Bent over my fence, Sallie twisted his neck and yelled back at me. "This ain't shit, C. Just a fight between brothers, I'll be out in no time."

The two big cops, breathing heavily, forced my brother down on the fence and then turned toward me.

I staggered to my feet. "He's got a previous for assault," I said. "Did eight years."

"Depends on the judge," the red-faced cop said, "but that

should get him back in for a little bit, this was assault, no doubt, and definitely aggravated."

I caught my breath and spoke very slowly through the pain. "A lawyer told me at least fifteen. Considering it's a second offense."

The cops nodded at the possibility as they fought against my brother's increasing resistance.

"What about possession?" I asked. "I heard they throw on more for that."

"Depends on the drug," Will's man said. "But that would add something for sure."

"Check his leather jacket, front right pocket," I said. "There's two crack vials in there."

Both cops widened their eyes and looked at me with surprise.

"And a gun in his other pocket," I added.

The cops freaked at the news of a gun and rushed to yank Don's gift of a pistol from my brother's front pocket. Sallie erupted, lurching back and sending the red-faced cop to the ground. The gun skipped across the sidewalk. Will's man scrambled for it. Sallie turned and curled into a fist with his arms behind his back. He torpedoed himself in my direction, screaming like a jet engine. The neighbors gasped as my brother came at me, the two cops in pursuit. As Sallie lunged at my sternum, I slipped to the side, like a bullfighter. As he hurtled by, the two cops tackled him to the ground. Then in tandem, they yanked my brother up by the cuffs and herded him towards the car. After a fierce struggle, they finally crammed him into the back seat and slammed the door. The car rocked from inside with Sallie's rage. He bashed his head, over and over, into the tinted window. "This ain't over. This ain't over, C," he screamed. "I ain't done with you!"

The two cops were pissed and ready to leave. "You should

have told us about that gun!" Will's man said.

"It's not loaded," I said.

"You sure?"

"I'm sure," I said. "Couldn't afford the bullets."

Will generously shook hands with both men, and offered soothing words as he led them to their vehicle. They climbed in their car and drove my brother away. He screamed at me from the back window, things cruel and threatening, but his words didn't matter to me anymore. I'd won. Like Finn McCool from my father's stories, I'd defeated the giant by biting off its finger.

Silence returned to the block, though most of my neighbors stayed where they were, talking quietly to one another.

"You a slick motherfucker," Will said. "You know that, Stiles?"

"Yeah," I said, wiping a streak of blood off my face with a sleeve. "Real slick."

I sat down on the stoop and lit a cigarette, feeling the burn in my chest in the now quiet afternoon. The neighbors started filtering away. Will spoke quietly with a few of them, introducing himself with great charm. Somewhere, on a distant block, a bat clattered off the asphalt.

When he was done talking with the neighbors, Will came over and shook my hand. He said that we had a deal, and that he'd be in touch soon. Before I went inside, I gave him the rest of the information I had on the Montclair Corporation, along with the business card of Andy Alvino.

**

Up on my roof, I let the late afternoon sun shine down on my battered body as I thought about that summer day ten years ago. There had been three of us—me, Angie, and his girlfriend at the time, a girl from town with straight yellow hair and a grape-colored birthmark splashed down one of her cheeks. We'd sneaked into the pool on the rich side of town, but had gotten ourselves kicked out for horseplay and cursing. With nothing to do, we hung around the parking lot, chucking bottles and rocks over the fence. A couple of older kids came out in bathing suits. They looked at the cutoffs we were wearing and said that we were dirty and that we smelled. We laughed. Then they made fun of my long hair and called me a queer.

Angie stepped up to one of the kids and punched him in the face, knocking him to the ground. That was how it worked. Angie was cool, until someone started with me. I could take care of myself, but he wouldn't let me. We figured that was that, but the kid got up and clocked Angie in the eye. Rich kids weren't supposed to know how to fight. Off balance at the unexpected assault, Angie's punches back were wild and off the mark, and the other kid took him until the people who ran the pool came out and broke it up. We walked home in silence.

By the tracks, Angie's eye swelled up and his lip grew fat. That's all it took for him to crack. All that pressure at home, especially after our father had vanished, must have turned his jaw to glass, and that rich kid had broken it like a bottle. Angie raged, said he was sick of sticking up for me, sick of sticking up for all of us. I'd never seen him so mad. His girlfriend tried to calm Angie down. He kept turning away, but she wouldn't let him. Secretly, she told him something he didn't want to hear, and he hit her across the face with an open hand as a train rattled by.

Tears gathered in the swollen saddle under my brother's eye, and he ran down the tracks. He talked about running away all the time, to faraway places like Florida and California, and said he was going to take me with him. I followed close behind, panting as I ran. I finally caught up to him in the valley. A train whistle blew as we wrestled on the landing along the cyclone fence of a scrap metal yard. Gravel tumbled down the ridge. I held my brother by the legs, squeezing for dear life, begging him not to go, not to leave without me. The whistle blew again. Angie pried himself free and started to run when a snarling German Sheppard watchdog smashed into the fence. Its growl and impact waylaid Angie; the gravel gave way under his feet. He clawed at the ridge as he tumbled towards the tracks, where the passing commuter train sucked him under.

His body contorted under the wheels, mangled into grotesque shapes as his screams disappeared into the pines. Limbs came out in pieces from under the belly of the passenger cars as the brakes screeched along the rails. Blood covered the tracks. When the train stopped, I ran into the woods and didn't stop until I came out on the other end, two towns away, disoriented and muddy, covered in burs and scratched to pieces. I'd broken an ankle but didn't remember how. Someone drove me home. The town cops were gathered in our living room while Sallie threw things around and put his fist through a wall and my mother wailed and wailed and wailed until a medic had her held down and put a needle in her arm. Later that night, from a hospital bed with my leg in a cast, I told the police that I had been too far away to have had anything to do with what happened. No one had seen me on top of that ridge wrestling with Angie, and I needed to keep it that way.

With Sallie gone, I could now finally face the truth. I hadn't killed my brother, but I had been there when he died, and for that, I'd secretly punished myself for the past decade. I decided that I wasn't going to do that to myself any longer.

Twilight began to settle as I sat on my roof under the Brooklyn sky and cried for my dead brother. Then I went to bed and breathed in the smell of Colette that was all over my sheets.

**

According to the Captain, the night before Easter was a big deal at the Notch, the night when everyone—the old-school crowd, the players, the young up-and-comers, and the regular folk from around the way, as he would say—stepped out to celebrate together. We had spoken for weeks about doing something different for the menu, and the Captain eventually agreed to my plan for a five course prix fixe, one seating, semi-formal dress, reservations required. The menu was posted on the wall two weeks in advance, and within a day, the books were full. The atmosphere was to be elegant, and for the food, I had decided on Creole—a grand cuisine with African and European roots.

Extra staff was hired, so I had help in the kitchen peeling and cleaning the shrimp, chopping vegetables for *miripoix*, and stirring flour and fat into a deep-brown roux. The last course was left to me alone, and I spent my prep-time working the bones out of a half dozen ducks. Downstairs, the Captain helped Jackie pop corks on the special wine he had bought for the occasion. Cases of Prosecco rested on ice. The tables were moved together and set with three plates in each spot. Candles flickered.

The wait staff wore black pants and white dress shirts, the Captain a blue suit, a pork pie hat tilted back on his head. He greeted each guest as they walked through the door while Jacqui, in a form-fitting evening dress, fluttered around the room with a tray of champagne flutes. From the stereo, Ella and Louis sang a duet.

After an opening hour of canapés and oysters and shrimp in Remoulade sauce, everyone sat down for the main courses. Slaving over my ducks in the kitchen, I could hear the happy murmurs as people ate the seafood gumbo, which was stocked with shellfish, peppers and spice. The murmurs turned to hollers when the next course, a rabbit and sausage etouffee, hit everyone's plate. The smell of deep flavor filled the air, along with the sound of joyous voices and clanging silverware and glasses. The staff was in constant motion, back and forth between the kitchen and the main room—the magic hum of a bustling restaurant.

The next course involved a bit of theatre. Covered platters were placed in front of each patron. Then, in concert, the servers dramatically removed the silver tops, revealing, with a whoosh of steam, a sea of shrimp in a light red sauce, layered over a mound of white rice, topped by a rose I'd carved from a whole tomato. This was my take on Shrimp Creole, a bayou classic. Busy in the kitchen basting the main course, I heard a roar of surprise, followed by applause and exclamations.

The hum returned as I continued in the kitchen. With the bones I'd taken out of the ducks, I made a stock; from that stock, I made a reduction. From the reduction I made a glaze. With that glaze I shellacked the roasting ducks to a deep mahogany, then stuffed each duck's hollowed cavity with Jambalaya, a thick rice dish with heavy seasoning and crumbled Cajun sausage. For the final step, I surgically cut each duck into eight slices, held the body together, re-glazed one last time, and put them all back in the oven for a minute to seal.

When they were ready, the ducks were transferred to hot trays and carried down to the floor, where they were placed on people's plates. Then each waitress, using the serving utensil, tapped the duck on top. From the stairs I watched as the whole body folded open into slices, and the jambalaya poured out over the meat. Silence, followed by an ovation. I went back to the kitchen and smoked a cigarette by the vent.

For dessert, I served warm pecan pie with French vanilla ice cream on the side.

Once the meal was over, people crowded so deep in front of the bar that the nearby tables had to be cleared away. I removed my apron, and went down to help Jacqui tend. Behind the bar, I put some Zydeco on the stereo and started taking drink orders. Hats and jackets came off; shoes, too. Hair dropped, mine included. The music, a mix of accordion, drums, guitar and spoons on a washboard, grooved. The whole room followed along, leaping into motion.

A petite woman, with a streak of silver through her flowing dark hair, stood watching the scene and clapping her hands. I walked out from behind the bar and led her by the wrist to the dance floor. The other dancers paused momentarily at the strange sight, then urged us on. "Go on, boy!" they yelled. "Go on now!"

With both hands, I led the woman away and back to one side, then the other, bouncing on one foot all the while, just like Carmen had taught me. People then filled in around us, but left enough room for us to maneuver. We did standard steps, back and forth, with the occasional spin tossed in. I bounced with the music, ignoring the pain in my side. The woman's skirt twirled as I picked up the spins. Then, for the grand finale, I pulled her alongside me, slipped my hand around the small of her back and held her hip, flipping her into the air. She did a complete somersault and landed gracefully on her feet. She came right back to me, smiling, as the astonished crowd cheered.

When the song was over, I thanked her for the dance. Then I went back to the bar and resumed my role as a server and an observer, happy to have been part of the mix, if just for a moment.

\*\*

The last diner went home around midnight. However, there were still stacks of dishes to wash and pots to scrub in the kitchen, as well as tables to be broken down and returned to their regular spots in the main room. As a result, I wasn't done until nearly two. I was spent as I walked down the stairs, exhausted after a long week of high emotions and brutal beatings. Despite the pain I felt, inside and out, I felt good for the moment, satisfied at the success of the last two days.

The Captain waved me over to his table by the window. I was glad to be able to sit down and have a few drinks with him. The riot gate was at half-mast. Jacqui, the only other staff member still here, was busy re-racking wine glasses and champagne flutes, so I brought my own beer and a fresh cognac over to the Captain's table. His loosened his tie, pushed back his hat and relaxed in the glow of success.

"Goddamn, Stiles!" the Captain said as I joined him by the window. The street outside was dark and quiet; the Captain drunk and happy as I'd ever seen him. "We goddamn killed tonight! Didn't we now? Didn't we?"

I had to agree.

"And look at you, boy," he said, ignoring the purple bruises that covered my face, "out there like a fool! I'd never seen a white boy go like that." He pointed his finger at me. "You all right, Stiles. You all right."

Some liquor spilled from his snifter, and he wiped it up with a stained handkerchief. I leaned back and took a big sip from my beer. The ale tasted like bitter honey, and the whole bottle went down in a few gulps. I got up and went behind the bar to get another beer, and put on some Jimmy Reed, the bouncing blues matching our ebullient mood. I returned with a fresh beer and the bottle of Cognac. The Captain bobbed his head to the music.

"And what are you doing for Easter?" I asked him.

"What's that now?" He responded, a surprised look on his face.

"Easter," I asked again. "You doing anything?"

"Not much, really," he said, absently scratching his crown. "Think I'll take a lady friend for a boat ride after church, maybe picnic over on Governor's Island."

"Which lady?" I asked.

"Don't know yet," he answered.

We laughed. I refilled his glass.

"Got a church in mind?" I asked.

"Baptist," he said, casting a look out the window. "Over there."

"I didn't know you were a church goer?"

"Yeah, well, the reverend and her deacons been on me for a while, and I figured it's about time I got right with God, before it's too late." He knocked back the booze, and banged the bottom of his glass on the table. I filled him up again. Outside, a sheath of newspaper rattled over the sidewalk like urban tumbleweed.

"Best get going before this rain hits," the Captain advised, taking a sip from the two fingers I had just poured. Heavy-bellied clouds had been rolling in all evening. We stared at the street in silence until an unexpected question, like a sneeze, shot from my mouth.

"Cyrus all right with God?" I asked.

The Captain smacked his hand on the table. "The hell you talking about? Why you asking about him?" His voice was deeper than usual, and the booze made his eyes glassy and unsteady as he struggled to stare me down.

I said nothing and lit a cigarette. The air had grown thick from the impending rain. Condensation collected and streamed down the cold beer bottle. In the silence, a long ash grew on the end of my cigarette, then broke off and dropped to the table.

The Captain kept his eyes on me until his mouth could no longer stay closed.

"The hell you going with this, Stiles?"

"I just want to know if someone like Cyrus can get right with God just by showing up at church on Sunday. He must have to sing in the choir or something."

"The hell do you know about him anyway? The hell you know about anything?"

I told him I knew Cyrus was running an orphan scam, collecting money from the city for housing foster kids, who were selling drugs and skipping school and fathering children. I also told him how he had tried to force me into hiring the silent man. I left it at that, though I could have told the Captain that I knew he was connected to all of it, laundering money through the Notch, loan sharking and collecting property. I could have told him that I also knew that he was the Claire in Montclair Corporation, and that Claire Horton and Montgomery Ratchford owned twenty-eight buildings, a restaurant, a laundry, a hardware store, and a check cashing place. I could have told the Captain everything I knew, but that information didn't belong to me anymore—I'd sold it to Will in exchange for the help with his cop friends. So I left it at Cyrus.

The Captain shifted on his seat and leaned towards me. "So goddamn what about Cyrus and all his business? You think you know something? Hell, this ain't middle America, boy, or wherever the hell you from. It ain't Manhattan either—this is Brooklyn, real motherfucking Brooklyn, and we got our own rules round here, our own way of living, our own way at looking at things. I don't worry 'bout no one's business, no one worries 'bout mine. You got eyes, Stiles. You see people coming in here before we open. So what? Someone needs money, I lend it to them without that inflated interest the Jews charge. I know it ain't legal, but it's right. We a community here, and we look out for one another cause no one else will."

He knocked back the rest of the Cognac in his glass, and jutted his chin towards the bottle. I filled him up again. He wiped the side of his mouth with the back of his jacket sleeve, nodded towards my pack of smokes. I extended him the open box, lit the cigarette once it was in his mouth. "Thanks," he said, jetting smoke through his nose. He looked down at the table and shook his head, slowly at first, then faster until he worked up some steam. He dropped the cigarette to the floor and stomped it out.

"One thing's for sure—we got the right to do whatever the fuck we please. All the bullshit we black folk have had to deal with. All the struggles. Shit, Stiles, you ain't know shit about that, white boy like you. Hell, my father's father was a slave. And my father grew up in a shack, four goddamn walls of wood. Son of a sharecropper. He don't done take a shit on a working toilet until he was fifteen years old, after he come on up here from Virginia for a decent job. His daddy worked on them boats, twelve hours a day, until they sent him off to die for a country where he ain't even a man. Then my daddy has to take care of his whole family. Started working on them ships, too, at sixteen years old, and he didn't stop until they shut that yard down, sent all them jobs back down to Virginia. Ain't that a bitch? The man probably figured too many black folk making a decent living. But we keep at it, that's for sure. My daddy started this here bar, made a place for black folk to come out and hear some music, drink, be together, enjoy life a little bit, once in a while. Yeah, we a resilient bunch of people and we always work and we find a way to keep our homes, our neighborhood. No matter, we keep on, through it all, and generations come up round here, in these same houses, on these same streets, and no matter what, we have our homes, our streets. This is ours, our place, and nobody can take that as long as we got ownership, and that's what we do, really—we in the ownership business. We buy up homes that people might lose, or lend some money to keep them from foreclosure or selling out. We charge fair rents, low interest, and keep them properties clean and safe, but not so clean and safe that outsiders come sniffing around.

"It ain't easy. People tempted by money, especially those who ain't never had none, and they're bloodsuckers everywhere, like your friend, that pretty boy, the only color he care about is green. Shit, I got a mind to eliminate his ass, and I tell you, ten, fifteen years ago, he'd been in the ground for his treachery, but we got to be careful now. Things creeping in, changing, white folks coming and we got to be smart in order to hold on. We like the fucking Indians—white man coming to take our land. But we gotta fight, boy. We gonna fight, too. Ain't no *Kimosabe* shit round here."

The Captain leaned back in his chair once he was done. Jacqui came up and stood behind him, her hands resting gently on his shoulders, her eyes staring down at me with contempt.

"And so that explains what Cyrus does?" I asked.

"Shit," the Captain said with a wagging finger, "I've done known him since he was a boy. He ain't perfect, but I tell you one goddamn thing, Stiles—not you, or nobody else, got the right to question him. No sir. You ain't got no right to question any of us. You've done give up that right. You just mind you own while living round here, and especially when you taking money from this motherfucking hand."

Jacqui nodded, said "Um-hmm," and squeezed the Captain's shoulder.

I finished my beer and dropped the cigarette in the bottle. "That how it works?"

"Damn right," the Captain said. He knocked his glass on the table and motioned towards the bottle. He had a fight coming, but it wasn't with me. I got up, walked out the door and ducked under the gate, followed the wind blowing towards home.

\*\*

On the dark, empty streets, the crisp wind punched my chest and burned my eyes. The sky hung low as I crossed under the yellow halos of street lights, my boots stomping the sidewalk. A drop of rain split the leaves and landed on my head like a dart.

Even before it had begun, I knew that tonight would be my last night at the Notch. It was time to move on. The past week of events and memories and dreams had made me realize that Brooklyn would never be my home. I had no interest arguing it out with the Captain, no desire to impress upon him my hard-earned wisdom, no desire whatsoever to do anything but face the facts of my life. I felt weightless and hollow, spooned clean by time. My mother was a breeze in the leaves of a tree; my dead brother a reflection in passing car windows; my father a voice in every story or song I heard. My decade of wandering since leaving the house I had grown up in had been an attempt to find a place of my own, a gesture of hope that had left me just as hopeless and alone as I had been ten years ago. And though I was worn down like an old coin by travel and constant readjustment, I again felt the road beckoning.

I was a block from my house when the downpour began, hard and heavy.

*Sunday*

I woke to the sound of church bells washing down the block in waves. I got out of bed and looked outside. The storm had scrubbed everything clean. The sky was bright blue and the buildings basked in the soft light of a new day. The house across the street was quiet: no noise, no activity, no rusty Continental. No one lived there anymore, it seemed.

I took a long bath in salted water, the fog around my head slowly lifting in the warm mist. I washed myself carefully, then bandaged my wounds. In the clean light of my room, I put on my best shirt and pants. Out front, the wooden stoop was still damp from the rain.

I rolled my shirtsleeves to the elbow, and picked lint off my pants as families passed on their way to church, the men wearing pinstriped suits, the women colorful dresses with glorious hats. Little boys wrestled within their formal clothes, and the girls clutched corsages to their lace-draped chests. I smiled and nodded at my neighbors; they returned the gesture in kind. This had always been the extent of my contact with my neighbors—a smile and a nod. I wondered if they simply thought I was fixing the house for somebody else. No matter what, I must have been an enigma to them, a white boy with long hair who kept odd hours. I had lived on this block for a year, but I only knew one person by name.

I rang Angel's bell. After a minute, she appeared in the doorway under the stairs, struggling with an earring. "Oh, hi Caesar," she said. "I thought you were somebody else." She wore a sleeveless yellow dress, tight around her torso and blossoming out below her narrow waist. A string of pearls circled her neck. The smell of hyacinth filled the vestibule.

I extended a dusty bottle of wine.

"What's this?" she asked.

"An Easter gift," I said, still holding the bottle. "It's an Italian wine I'd been saving."

"That's sweet," she said, in a way that wasn't so sweet. "But I don't drink wine."

I pulled back the bottle.

"No," she said, matter of fact. "I don't touch alcohol or meat of any kind."

"Good thing I didn't invite you over for Easter," I said.

"Good thing," she said with a smile, until her brows knitted in concern. "What happened to your face?"

I tongued my broken tooth and told her I had fallen down the stairs. She pinched her lips in doubt then began fussing with her earring again. Her raised eyebrows asked me if there was anything else. I handed her a legal envelope.

"What's this?"

"I'm selling the house."

Oh, no," she said. "What does that…"

I held up a hand. "You have nothing to worry about. In the envelope is an open-ended lease. You can stay as long as you like. Rent goes up 3 percent every two years."

She did the math. "That's it? You sure?"

I nodded.

"Thank you, Caesar," she said warmly.

I nodded again.

"When will all this take effect?" she asked.

"I'm leaving today."

"Oh," she said, a hand to her mouth. "What about your things?"

"I don't really have much," I said, "just some clothes and a painting. Someone will be by in a few days to pick it all up. There's an address in the envelope where you can send your checks for now. When the sale closes, in six weeks or so, you'll meet the new owner. His name is William Page."

Angel frowned, maybe saddened for a moment with a passing regret that we didn't get a chance to know each other better. Probably for the best—there's no way I'd last with a woman who didn't touch alcohol or meat of any kind. I shook her hand, wished her well, and told her goodbye.

**

I walked down the block as the pigeons flipped overhead and morning glories bloomed in front gardens. Children, careful of their church clothes, played gently out front as they waited on their parents. I turned off the block and walked the peaceful streets of the neighborhood. The sun was warm and abundant. Passing the church, I heard "The Welcome Table" being belted out by the choir and the full house of worshipers. The mighty church seemed to move. I was sure that Macie Turner knew that song, and I imagined him inside, swaying with the Reverend and her deacons and the whole congregation in their weekly moments of grace, letting the gospel of the blues help them understand life. I wondered if the Captain, sitting inside the church, knew what had happened to Cyrus yet. I wondered if today would be the day that he got right with God. I wondered if he knew on whom the devil prays, and that his Brooklyn—*real motherfucking Brooklyn*—was full of unloved children.

On the commercial strip, the stores were mostly closed. The riot gate was down at The Notch. I walked the streets alone, past the park and the projects, along the main road into downtown and beyond to the busy arteries and byways that feed the tunnels and bridges that brought people in and out of the remarkable borough of Brooklyn. Traffic moved peacefully along.

I crossed the wide street and walked the bridge my grandfather's grandfather had come here to build. He escaped from the poverty of Italy and settled in a strange land with a strange language, and had made a life for himself. And the tribute to his triumph spans a river. It was an example I decided to embrace, his legacy to follow.

With my knife, I sliced off the foil on the bottle of wine and pried out the cork. On the landing in the middle of the Brooklyn Bridge, the warm sun on my face, over the traffic and the rushing river, between the skyline of lower Manhattan and the corridors of Brooklyn, with the islands and the boats and the Statue of Liberty in the wide harbor that opens to the world like the arms of America, I drank the wine and toasted a story—my future—that had yet to be told.

Then I walked over the rest of the bridge into Manhattan. I caught the subway, then a Jersey bound train back to the town where I was born, to live in my childhood house and buy that old inn, determined to make a home of my own, and in the process, break the curse of my mother's mother who came to this country in the usual way.

## Acknowledgements

I am indebted and thankful to The New School's MFA in Creative Writing program. Special thanks to all of my instructors and classmates, particularly my adviser Patrick McGrath and my dear friends Carlos Dews, Steven Estok, and Becky Ferreira for their insightful critiques and tireless support. My agent Jennifer Carlson deserves thanks for finding the manuscript a great home. And thanks to Robert and Elizabeth at Ig Publishing for their belief in the story and all the work required to turn my pages into this novel.